WHISPERING THOUGHTS

Air Marshal A V Vaidya PVSM, VM (Retd.)

Email vaidyaajit@yahoo.com

Creative CROWS
PUBLISHERS LLP
the publishing & communication people

Published by

Office : D-328, Defence Colony, New Delhi-110024
Mobiles: +91-9810539784, +91-9833283155
Emails: ganivpanjrath@yahoo.co.in, tannaazirani@gmail.com

ISBN-13: 978-81-944786-7-6
ISBN 10: 81-944786-7-7

MRP: Rs. 315/-

Printed at Thomson Press, New Delhi

INTRODUCTION

I have written this small book not as one story but as a collection of small stories derived from my experiences during my life of seventy odd years. It is sort of a follow up of my earlier published book "Aboard my Rocking Chair". I find that most readers are quite scared of picking up huge, fat story books primarily because in today's world scenario most people don't have adequate time to give to their family members leave aside reading. It is quite like preferring to watch a T-20 Cricket Match rather than a Test Match. Though I am retired and have lot of time, I experience similar feeling when I visit the library. Another thing that I look for is a nice big font which puts less pressure on my eyes and brain. I think you will find reading this book quite interesting, enjoyable and also educative and you may like to derive your own lessons which may help you to live your life more comfortably.

Contents

CHAPTER 1

MY FIGHT WITH CANCER

Being in the Air Force and that too a Fighter Pilot, I had to compulsorily go through a proper comprehensive medical examination every year. During the annual medical in Dec 2004 it was detected that I have cancer. You may like to know how I handled this situation and derive some lessons from it.

Well, frankly I found it very difficult to believe that cancer has got me. Somehow, all along I felt that nothing serious like cancer or heart attack can ever happen to me. Such things were meant for those who hadn't been leading a disciplined life. A fellow like me who had been trained in the National Defence Academy and who had led an active life and had played games all along and done lot of exercising and regular walking, certainly can't be penalized with something like cancer.

There must be some mistake in the diagnosis I thought. Frankly it took quite a while for this information to sink in my brain. But when it did sink in, I took it quite philosophically like I had taken many other failures and shocks earlier in my life as a fighter pilot. I also realised that there is no proper logic when it comes to heart attacks, strokes and cancer. These things can happen to anybody and at any time.

After my mind accepted that I had got cancer, I said to myself, "No, I am not going to buckle down under the pressures of cancer so easily. After all, I am a soldier and I must FIGHT and set an example. My wife, my daughters, my mother, all my relatives, my oncologists and this entire Indian Air Force is with me in this fight - how can I let them down?". Everyone knows that life is full of ups and downs and that the real test comes when one goes down. That's when one has to fight and show adequate courage to come up again. My wife, and my Staff Officer (then Wing Commander Hanspal) helped me a great deal to put up a brave fight.

R & R (Research and Referral) hospital where I was being treated helped me a great deal in strengthening my resolve to put up a good fight. When I used to take walks in the corridors of the hospital, I used to see many patients, some badly burnt cases, some with one leg amputed, some with even both legs gone, some with an eye lost, but they never let their smile go. I also saw cancer struck children just about 5,6 years young happily bouncing around and playing and I used to wonder what those poor kids have done to deserve cancer. Looking at them my resolve used to get strengthened. I used to think, if they can fight without losing their smile, why can't I?

To most people, cancer spells death but my mind somehow refused to give this meaning to cancer. Hope is something fantastic. It can bias and change one's thinking completely towards positive side and my mind certainly was tilted in that direction. They said that positive thinking is very important in cancer cases like mine and somehow my mind was already doing so without much of prompting.

I was convinced that fighting cancer was more a mind game than medical game. And well, thanks to my oncologists and all those who were with me and helping me to fight this battle, though it took over a year, I won the battle and re-joined my duties as Deputy Chief. For further information you may like to read my book titled "Got Cancer – Don't Worry" which I wrote while undergoing treatment. Contact me on my email and I will send it to you.

CHAPTER 2

GALAT NAMUNA

During my service in the Indian Air Force for 39 odd years, I came across many bosses – some good, some bad and some even ugly. But I must confess that I got to learn a lot from all of them. Some taught me the right way by setting good examples and some the wrong way by setting bad examples. I feel that one learns more from a bad example.

When I was a cadet in the National Defence Academy, I remember how I was taught Boxing. It was taught to us using "Sahi Namuna" meaning correct way of boxing and then "Galat Namuna" meaning wrong way. And I still remember how the "Galat Numana" was more effective and how it has remained stuck in my head even today. Similarly the bad and ugly bosses taught me a lot more than the good ones. They taught me what not to do while the good ones taught me what I should do.

Let's take an example. A good Boss always comes on time for work and clears all his files on time. He sets a very good example to learn from. On the contrary, there is another Boss who chooses to come to office whenever he feels like just because he is the Boss. His IN Tray of files is never empty. The files move very slowly in his office. Lesson to be learnt from both the Bosses is same – "Always come to work on time and do your job promptly". Who do you think has conveyed this lesson more effectively?

Watching the Bad bosses I often used to make a mental note of what I will not do if ever I become a Boss. I will certainly not behave the way one of the bad Bosses was behaving for example, "Shouting at a subordinate in front of his juniors", or "Calling somebody to the office and keeping him waiting outside for an hour, thus wasting his time", or "Taking advantage of one's position and not paying one's personal bills, for example Mess Bill".

Yet another Boss who taught me how not to behave was a short tempered fellow who believed in "No nonsense". He wanted everything, big or small, done exactly the way he wanted. He gave no space to his subordinates to think. He killed their initiative totally. He used to shout and create a phobia around him. Out of fear, those working under him used to reach a stage when they used to sit with folded hands and do nothing unless told by him. What an excellent example of "Galat Namuna" he was!!

Then there was a Boss who was very scared of taking a decision. Before taking a decision, he would consult number of subordinates. He was mighty scared of "What will people say, if the decision goes wrong?". He was always looking for cheap popularity. As a result of delayed decisions, the progress in work was also slow. Contrary to this Boss, there was another Boss who didn't bother to consult anybody and took a decision based on what he felt was right. Two out of ten times, may be, he was wrong but overall work under him progressed at a good speed. I liked working under him.

Then there was another variety of Boss. His juniors used to call him mad. He suffered from "Zero Error Syndrome". Out of ten things, even if one thing was not done as per his satisfaction, he used to blast that individual and not mention anything about the nine things which were done well – crazy fellow.

Well, world is full of all kinds of people – Good, Bad and even Ugly. God decides what kind of people come your way. Your job is to stay calm and cool and learn from all of them because these lessons which they give will make you a better human being. God Bless.

<u>CHAPTER 3</u>

<u>LIFE AFTER RETIREMENT</u>

When I was in active service, my day was jam packed from morning till night. I didn't have even a minute for myself. Time seemed to pass so quickly that before I realised it would be time for dinner. But when I retired, I found that I was surrounded by vacuum on all sides. Time hung on me and I didn't know what to do with it. That is when it struck me that I must Plan my day. No point getting up at any odd time and dragging myself through the day.

So, what should I do? How do I start my day? I realised that now that we don't have enough help in the form of servants, I must do all my jobs myself like setting the bed, tiding the room and so on and that will also help me to pass my time. I must set my alarm to six-o-clock and must get out of bed when it rings and not laze around.

What next? I love to play Golf so why not go for Golf followed by breakfast in the club at least on alternate days. That will take care of three hours. What about the other alternate days? Well, I could do Yogasanas and breathing exercises like Pranayam and follow it up with a nice walk in fresh air for an hour and finally have a soothing bath. That should take me to around nine thirty - breakfast time. I could earn a plus point from my wife by making breakfast for both of us!

What next? Well, read the newspaper, catch up with the latest news and then sit on the computer. Go through the emails and other massages, do some reading and writing which I am fond of and then follow it up with buying and selling of Shares. I had decided to keep aside Rs 30,000/- for dabbling in Stock Market. In doing so, idea was not to make money but just to pass time. I found this very interesting and it would take me to lunch time.

What after lunch? Well, a short nap to get my energy level to normal and then what? This problem was solved by my wife. She has done post-graduation in Mathematics and Statistics and she loves teaching mathematics. She started her Maths classes for students of 9th and 10th in the afternoons at four-o-clock after the children finished their school by around three-o-clock. The parents wanted children to be taught Science also (Physics, Chemistry and Biology). I told my wife that I can handle that. So classes took my time to around six-o-clock. Spending time in the evening was never a problem for me. I could comfortably spend time watching games on TV or socialising with friends or watching a movie. That took care of rest of the day. So, I had succeeded in planning my routine. Now all I had to do was stick to it so that time doesn't hang on me.

It is said that vacant mind is a devil's workshop. This plan will ensure that this doesn't apply to me. Planning how to spend one's day is extremely important for all whether working or retired, whether old or young. One must also set some small goals to be achieved in a week or a month like dropping a stroke from one's golf handicap or finish reading a book by month end or reducing a Kg by exercising in a set period and so on. And it is also important to regurgitate the day's happenings. Before falling asleep, while in bed, one must think of the day's happenings. Did I stick to my plan? Did I achieve what I had planned? If not, where did I fail? Based on this, one must plan the next day. Doing this will also give you good sleep.

CHAPTER 4

PRINCIPLES OF FAMILY WAR

One often gets to hear this ironical statement that nothing is constant other than change. Time moves on bringing changes in our daily life and in the global environment. With these changing situations one needs to review ones thought process and action plans to deal with the changed scenario. Short skirts seemed provocative to the previous generation but they look smart to the future generation – a case of change in thinking process with passage of time.

Based on the understanding of old wars, a gentleman named Clausewitz articulated certain Principles which, if adhered to in war, improved the probability of success. These became very famous and got to be known as "Principles of War". But with changing scenarios, some feel that these Principles have become outdated and irrelevant and need to be reviewed.

Thinking of these Principles of War, I was struck with a crazy idea – Why not enumerate certain statements and call them "Principles of Home War" which if adhered to, might give a better chance to the husbands to survive in their home wars against their wives!

I don't think that in any marriage, husband and wife live "happily ever after" without quarrelling. In day to day life, there are many instances which result in difference of opinion or difference in understanding of a situation which often give rise to loud bouts of verbal war. I found that this is very common and unavoidable situation in every marriage and it gets worse as years roll on.

Talking of middle class marriages, things were different few generations before when women were not permitted to have an opinion on any subject or situation. But with passage of time, things have changed. Most women of middle class are now educated. They marry late compared to the women of yester years. This delay in marriage often results in these women developing a fixed set of mind which they don't want to change after marriage. Also their tolerance level has gone down, more so because they are earning good amount of money which has also given them higher level of independence. All these changes put together have increased the conflicts between husband and wife. On drop of a hat, the fights start and tempers run high. These fights are further aggravated by low tolerance levels. All this has appreciably increased the divorce rate.

The two statements that I want to put across as Principles of Family War are intended to reduce fights, reduce divorces and being a man myself, hope that they will help husbands to survive better because I have noticed that the attrition rate of husbands in these family wars is rather high.

<u>First Principle</u> :- In a marriage war, I have yet to see a husband winning. All my golfer friends agree with me hundred percent. So, in any argument, start with the assumption that it is a losing war that you are fighting and then be sensible enough to tell yourself that why fight at all? But not saying a few words may not give you joy so take the

fight to a certain enjoyable level and having angered your wife just below the level beyond which she starts throwing things, shut your mouth. I have seen that most wives want and love to fight. So, as a good husband, give her that chance and let her feel happy that she has won the war – call it sportsman spirit or whatever.

<u>Second Principle</u> :- English language has given us two wonderful words – "Sorry" and "OK". These words sort out many problems but unfortunately, in today's scenario these words are rarely used – specially the word "Sorry". The culprit is EGO. The Ego of a man does not permit him to say sorry. He has a mental block that by using the word sorry, he is demeaning himself in the eyes of his wife who might think that she is "one up" and take advantage of the situation. My advice to the husband is – say SORRY – if required, say SORRY ten times. Remember that you don't have to actually feel sorry!! Saying so will bring about a temporary "Truce" and you will live to fight yet another day. Finally and quietly do what you actually wanted to do.

I have experienced that many a times the wife blames the husband that he just sits and does nothing particularly after his retirement. She then orders him to do some work in a tone which is rather harsh. This angers the husband and he feels like rebelling. Well, if you want to have a fight, fine, go ahead, but my advice to you would be, just control your anger and say "OK". You would have saved at least half an hour of precious time. There can be many other occasions where the wife will use instigating sentences, my advice, "Control, Control" – just say "OK".

The summary of the Principles of Home War can be listed as follows :-

1. Remember that no husband has ever won this war.
2. Say Sorry at the opportune time.
3. Use the word OK to while away the situation.
4. But fight you must to derive some joy and to give your wife happiness of victory.

GOD Bless.

CHAPTER 5

FLATTERY

In today's scenario, life has become very competitive. As a result, getting promoted has become very tough. People are resorting to all kinds of strategies like demeaning one's contemporaries by telling the Boss negative things about them. Another way to supersede the contemporaries in the struggle for promotion is to "Buy the Boss" by treating him with lavish meals and flattering him no end so that it becomes embarrassing for him to deny promotion to you. Such people are commonly referred to as "Chamchas" in Indian parlance.

Flattery is as old as mankind. There are many examples of a mother flattering her child to get something done. "Drink this milk Beta. You are such a nice child. I will give you a chocolate if you finish this milk fast" – that's flattery and bribery used together. Someone has very beautifully said "Bribery and even Corruption starts at home, why blame elders" – How true!!

It is quite common for a wife to flatter her husband and having conquered his mind demand something valuable which she may not have got without flattering him. While dealing with Akbar, flattery was abundantly used by Birbal to stay away from his wrath. Most of the human beings are vulnerable to Flattery.

The basic question is - "Is Practice of Flattery Bad?" Well the answer can be YES and NO. A lot depends on the end intentions. If end intensions are bad, then flattery being the means to achieve that unjustified end would be bad. If the intentions are not going to cause harm to anyone then one may not call it bad. But many flatterers tend to become sycophants which is bad. They resort to flattery of the Boss to hide their weakness and faults and gain some advantage. They can be called as "Bootlickers" or "Chamchas". But genuine flattery with no selfish motive is indeed good and gets the person motivated to perform better. For instance, telling your subordinate, "Good job, Well done, You are Great, Keep it up".

The art of flattery is practised quite widely in almost all the professions. Some of the ways that come to mind in which flattery is used are for instance while playing games with the Boss. In Golf, all his shots are loudly proclaimed as "Great Shots". If his Putt doesn't sink, then it is said that it is because the grass on the putting green hasn't been cut properly. While playing Bridge, if the game is made, then it is loudly said, "What excellent Calls you made Sir". In the game of Squash he is always made to win. In parties his predecessor is subtly demeaned by saying how he never bothered about the welfare of his employees subtly implying what a better leader he is. His wife is also not spared. She is invariably made to win in the game of Tambola. She is highly praised for her choice of Sarees and how graceful and dignified she looks in them. The Boss enjoys this flattery. Idea of the smart junior in this flattery game is to get a good annual report so that his promotion prospects get better. Is this justified? What do you have to say?

CHAPTER 6

BODY & SOUL

While I was in Service, I happened to go to Mount Abu where I got a chance to visit Brahma Kumari Organisation. I had no idea about what that Organisation does except that it deals with spiritual aspects. As I entered the Organisation, I was warmly received by a gentleman. Probably he knew that I was a senior officer in the Indian Air Force. He said, "Sir, please follow me, I will take you around the Organisation and tell you what it does".

The first place he took me to was a huge hall called the Meditation Hall. There he said, "Sir, do you mind if I ask you a question?" I replied, "Yes, please go ahead". He said, "Sir, please tell me – Who are YOU?" to which I replied, "I am Air Commodore Ajit Vaidya". He again piped up, "No Sir, Who are YOU?" I again replied, "I am an Air Force officer and a Fighter Pilot". He again pestered me with the same question, "Sir, WHO ARE YOU?"

Well I ran out of patience and said, "Sorry, I don't know who I am, please tell me". Very patiently he said, "Sir, I will tell you who you are. You are a SOUL with a BODY named Vaidya to carry you around. When this BODY gets old and tattered, YOU meaning the SOUL will leave this BODY and enter into another BODY with another name. This BODY called Vaidya is temporary and perishable while your SOUL is immortal and permanent. In Geeta this concept has been beautifully explained in two verses – One verse states that the SOUL cannot be destroyed by any Weapon, Fire cannot burn it, Water cannot dissolve it and neither can Wind dry it. The other verse states that just as a person gets rid of his garment (for example a shirt) when it gets tattered and torn because of usage over a period of time, similarly the owner of the BODY, the SOUL, abandons the BODY when it gets old and tattered and enters into a new BODY. Though perishable, it is our duty to look after our BODY because it is the carrier of our SOUL and we own it".

He then took me to Prayer Room, Library which had large number of books and a sound proof Reading Room, Dining Hall etc all the time talking to me at spiritual level. Well, when I came out of that Organisation, I was a changed man. The visit had certainly made me think that I must not abuse my BODY by over drinking, smoking and by other bad habits. I was reminded of the rule of moderation. It states that no need to be a Saint, enjoy your life given to you by GOD, enjoy the various pleasures that life offers but do everything in MODERATION.

CHAPTER 7

GOING TO AMERICA - WATCH OUT

My wife and I have been visiting US and UK number of times because, after their marriage, one of our daughters took citizenship of US and the other one of UK. Every visit of ours has taught us many things. We have been amazed to notice the various differences that exist in the style of living at US, UK and also India and we often get confused.

America is a much younger country and was discovered in 1492 by Christopher Columbus and there after migration started in a big way from Spain, Portugal and later from England and France. This led to a cultural transformation in many spheres. The English language was first introduced to America by British colonization. The formalisation of the differences in pronunciation and spellings in English language between US and UK came from Noah Webster who wrote the first American Dictionary published in 1828 with the intention of showing that people in the United States spoke a different dialect from Britain.

Many differences came about just to show that US is a different country and has its own different ways of doing things. Since US is much younger, people often say that things are done the wrong way in US. For example an electric switch when put down is ON in UK but it is OFF in US. In a three pin plug, earth hole is on top in UK while in US it is at the bottom. People drive cars on the left of the road in right hand driven vehicles in UK but in US it is the opposite. Vehicles are driven on the right side of the road in left hand driven cars. There are no roundabouts in crossing roads in US like there are in UK. Many more prominent and subtle differences are listed below which you may find quite interesting to read.

If you want to urinate then in UK you say you want to "wee" and not "pee" as in US and it is a "restroom" and not "toilet" as in UK. If you want to flush after doing your job then look for the flushing lever on left side in US and not on right as in UK. Everything is comparatively bigger in US. In UK the roads are small and the cars are also smaller. When greeting someone you say "you alright?" in US rather than "how are you?" as in UK.

Biscuits are essentially referred to as cookies in US. It's "jumpers" and not "sweaters" as in UK. In UK it's petrol, not gas, and it's sold by the litre not by gallon. "Full stop" is "Period" in US. The date is written as day, month, year in UK while in US month is written first and then day followed by year.

In UK they generally have separate boys and girls schools and the uniforms to go with them. While in US there is mostly co-education and no school uniforms. When asked why no uniforms, they say we don't want to cramp the freedom of children! In US there are "mailboxes" outside while in UK they have "letter boxes" built within the front door. Americans go on vacation, while Brits go on holidays. New Yorkers live in apartments; Londoners live in flats.

Americans spell the words as given to them in Webster's dictionary. Webster while making the dictionary dropped the letter "u" from many words to make the spelling match the pronunciation for example colour is color, honour is honor, labour is labor. Similarly there are different words for the same thing – Mom and Mum, Bar and Pub, Bum and Butt, Mail and Post and many more.

In a cooking gas burner, the knobs work differently. In UK or India, to put the gas ON you turn the knob anticlockwise and to put it off clockwise. It is reverse in US. To put the gas ON, the knob has to be turned clockwise and to put it off, anticlockwise. Coming from UK/India one has to be careful while working in the kitchen in US.

Another amazing thing we encountered in US was the Bus Service run by the Chinese to take visitors and show them around. We booked for one to take us to Washington, Philadelphia and Niagara Falls. It was a six days trip and the tickets were comparatively much cheaper but most amazing was the offer "Take two tickets and get one free". We jumped at it and our daughter could come with us free of cost and give us company. The trip was very well organized and also well executed. It stopped overnight at very good hotels and at places where we could enjoy eating the kind of food we wanted. Trust the Chinese!!

When one visits US, one notices that Americans like to live in Comfort and they are ready to work hard to achieve it and also to spend money for it. Everything is top class here and big like big houses, big cars, big roads. US is indeed a great country, it is a beautiful country, it is a very friendly country and an amazing amalgamation of many cultures. We really enjoy our trips to America.

CHAPTER 8

MORE ABOUT AMERICA

Summer was approaching and long awaited summer holidays were to start. My wife and I decided to go to America to visit our daughter and play with our granddaughters. Both the granddaughters are such darlings and we really derive immense happiness talking to them and playing with them. We were amazed to see that both of them besides getting A+ grades in their studies, take part in many other activities and some of them are really amazing like the elder one playing excellent competitive golf at the age of ten and the younger one playing ice hockey at the age of eight. Besides that they play piano, do difficult dance like Kathak and take part in competitive singing. America is great in this respect. They have created all the facilities for children to participate in many activities. They encourage catching children at a very young age and introducing them to various activities to produce champions. No wonder they win so many gold medals in Olympics.

One thing that we noticed in this visit was that Americans have left no stone unturned in replacing labourers with machines. They have shortage of labourers and that perhaps has driven them to invent machines to replace them. They have invented machines for practically everything for example for washing dishes, washing clothes and even drying them.

Americans also try and save body energy where ever they can. This time we were amazed to see that their tooth brush is also mechanized. One has to put the paste on the brush, put the brush on the teeth and put the switch ON and the brush vibrates and cleans the teeth. A simple thing like sharpening a pencil has also been mechanised. One has to put the pencil in the sharpener and put the switch on and the pencil gets sharpened.

Yet another very amazing thing we observed was the gadget that cleans the bottom after finishing the big job. It is attached to the pot. And after finishing the job all one has to do is to rotate the switch on the gadget and the gadget sends a jet of water directed on your anus and you are done.

One nice thing that we observed while watching the Ads on TV was about bearing the cost of your own funeral. The charges for coffin and subsequent ceremony are rather heavy in US and also in UK, so to avoid this burden of expenditure on the children, certain schemes have started which accept certain amount of money on a monthly basis. The accumulated money is then used to meet the expenditure for one's funeral.

A funeral plan allows you to freeze funeral costs at today's prices. It also contributes in helping to protect your family emotionally and financially when the time comes. Getting a funeral plan is a safe and easy way of giving a final parting gift to your loved ones, lending them a helping hand when they need it most. What an excellent idea!!

CHAPTER 9

SHANTA BAI

You must have guessed that Shanta Bai is the name of the maid who comes to do sweeping and swopping of our flat in India. She is an amazing lady - generally on time, fast and efficient. She is like a machine and goes house to house doing the same job leaving us wondering how she manages to do that. Her life story is very sad. She has four children. Her husband is a drunkard of the first order and does no work. He drinks from the money which Shanta Bai earns and if she does not give him the money, then he hits her till she is black and blue and all this in front of the children. Poor lady howls but no one comes to her help. Finally she got fed up and left him and went to her mother's place but he keeps coming back to extract some money out of her.

We advised her to launch a police complaint which she did after a lot of pursuing because she was scared to do so. Now the case is in the court for divorce. One wonders what will happen and how much money the lawyer will squeeze out of her. We help her monetarily as much as we can and perhaps that is why she is loyal to us.

The story of other maids who work in nearby flats is no different. Husbands of most of them are drunkards and almost all of them have separated from their husbands. Most of the other maids are not as efficient and punctual like

Shanta Bai. Many a times, they don't turn up and don't even inform that they are not going to come and later give some flimsy excuse. But whatever that be, they are still a great help.

One day while in a conversation in a party, I asked one lady that when the doorbell rings and you go to open the door, do you feel happier to see the maid or do you feel happier if you see your husband? Quite sheepishly and gingerly she answered in a low voice "of course the maid but don't tell that to my husband because he won't understand what hell I go through if she doesn't turn up."

In US where cheap labour is not easily available, Shanta Bai has been replaced by a mechanical gadget. It cleans the dust from the entire floor of the house. It is smart and most reliable. It is about one and a half feet long, one foot wide and six inches tall. One has to programme it. Set the start time eg 1200h and finishing time as 1300h and then exactly at 1200h it starts it's journey from it's home (corner where it is parked). When it encounters an obstacle like a wall, it turns and continues. Some other parameters are fed into it so that it cleans the rooms one by one as programmed. Basically it is a vacuum cleaner moving around and sucking all encountered dust and dirt and when its job nears its finishing time, it obediently returns to its home corner and switches off. We have named it Shantabai. What a wonderful gadget it is! - always on time, does an excellent job even when the owners are out of the house and gives no tension like the maid servants do by their irregular attendance and bad quality of work. Also, she is a spinster so no drinking problems!!

CHAPTER 10

TOUCHING STORIES

I would like to narrate some very heart touching stories which I happened to read after my retirement. They brought tears to my eyes. I think there is a lot to learn from them. These stories are short and sweet with a lot of meaning.

A soldier happened to visit a hospital to see one of his wounded friends. As soon as he entered the hospital, a nurse came running to him and said, "Please come. He has been waiting for you for a long time". The soldier could not say no. The nurse took him next to a bed on which an old man was breathing his last. The nurse brought a chair so that the soldier could sit beside the bed. All through the night the young soldier sat there in the poorly lighted ward, holding the old man's hand and offering him words of love and strength.

Occasionally, the nurse suggested that the soldier move away and rest for a while. He refused. Whenever the nurse came into the ward, the soldier was oblivious of her and of the night noises of the hospital. Now and then the nurse heard him say a few gentle words. The dying man said nothing all through the night to his son. He only held his hand tightly. Towards dawn, the old man died. The soldier released the now lifeless hand he had been holding and went to tell the nurse. While she did what she had to do, he waited.

Finally, she returned. She started to offer words of sympathy, but the soldier interrupted her. "Who was that man?" he asked. The nurse was startled, "He was your father", she answered. "No, he wasn't," the soldier replied. "I never saw him before in my life".

The nurse said, "Then why didn't you say something when I took you to him?" The soldier said, "I knew right away that there has been a mistake, but I also knew he needed his son and his son just wasn't here. When I realised that he was too sick to tell whether I was his son or not, knowing how much he needed me, I stayed."

What a heartwarming story!! The next time someone needs you, just be there - Stay. With passage of time most of us are becoming more and more selfish. We seem to have less time for anybody else. Even children are neglecting their parents during their old age – how sad !!

The next story is a short love story. This also has an important lesson. There was a blind girl who hated herself because of being blind. She hated everyone except her boyfriend. One day the girl said that if she can only see the world she will marry her boyfriend. One day someone donated eyes to her and then she could see everything including her boyfriend.

Her boyfriend asked her, "now that you can see, will you marry me?" The girl was shocked when she saw her boyfriend is also blind and she refused to marry him. Her boyfriend walked away with tears and said, "Just take care of my eyes dear".

What a touching story and how sad!! Well, you may draw your own conclusion and lessons. To me it appears like height of selfishness.

The next story is also short but sweet. A little girl and her father were crossing a bridge. The father was kind of scared so he asked his little daughter, "Sweetheart, please hold my hand so that you don't fall into the river." The little girl said, "No, Dad. You hold my hand." "What's the difference?" asked the puzzled father.

"There is a big difference," replied the little girl. "If I hold your hand and something happens to me, chances are that I may let your hand go. But if you hold my hand, I know for sure that no matter what happens, you will never let my hand go." What a beautiful reply. Please draw your own lessons.

The next story is also very interesting. One day, the father of a very wealthy family took his son on a trip to a nearby village with the specific purpose of showing him how poor people live. They spent a couple of days and nights as guests in a poor farmer's house.

On their return trip, the father asked his son, "How was the trip?" "It was great, Dad." The son replied. "Did you see how poor people live?" the father asked. "Oh yeah," said the son. "So, tell me, what did you learn from the trip?" asked the father.

The son answered: "I saw that we have one dog and they had four. We have a pool that reaches to the middle of our garden and they have a creek that has no end. We have imported lanterns in our garden and they have the stars at night. Our patio reaches to the front yard and they have the whole horizon. We have a small piece of land to live on and they have fields that go beyond our sight. We have servants who serve us, but they serve others. We buy our food, but they grow theirs. We have walls around our property to protect us, they have friends to protect them." The boy's father was speechless. Then his son added, "Thanks Dad for showing me how poor we are."

Isn't perspective a wonderful thing? I think we all should give thanks to God for everything we have, instead of worrying about what we don't have.

Hope you enjoyed the stories.

CHAPTER 11

FRIDAY DINNERS

Wow!! how we look forward to Friday Dinners! Because on Friday evenings a beautiful girl visits us and brings life into our home. Her Dad is a dear friend of mine who stays in some other town but her job demands that she stay away from them in some other town which happens to be where we stay. She is smart, she is sweet and she is very loving. She is like a daughter to both of us and floods our life with lots of love. Her name is Neha. She is a compulsive talker or should I say yapper! Out of the ten words spoken in the house after her arrival, eight or even nine belong to her. She generally doesn't pause when she is talking.

She fills the void created by our two daughters who left us years back after their marriage – one going to England and the other to America – never to return. Now we meet them during our or their yearly visits. But thanks to technology, we can see them and their children and have a nice chat on WhatsApp.

The Friday dinner menu is decided mainly by Neha. At times she brings butter chicken or some veg cooked by her or she requests my wife (Aunty for her) to cook a particular veg which she likes or even "Khichdi". Right from the time she enters the house, she starts looking for some work. She can't stay still. She is very restless. She wants to do everything. She wants me to just sit down, relax and enjoy my drink. She takes over all my jobs while I insist that she should relax and let me do my jobs. She doesn't let me set the table, fill water in the glasses etc. She just runs ahead of me and grabs the plates, glasses, spoons etc and then ends up giving me a big smile as if she has won the battle. And then she hovers around in the kitchen wanting to learn cooking from Aunty or pester her to get some job from her like cutting onions or tomatoes for salad. Needless to say, that her tongue is continuously busy saying something or the other.

Whenever my wife and I have a difference of opinion and the amplitude of our arguments starts rising she gives me a smile with a wink indicating that she is actually with me but smartly tells Aunty how right she is. I think she would have made a great politician.

I can't forget one incidence which I must narrate. One Friday when she visited us, she saw one glass bottle which she liked and wanted to take home. I told her that I will wrap it in old newspaper and give it to her. While I was doing that she came running and said, "Give me Uncle, I will wrap it". She almost snatched it from my hands and hurriedly did a bad job of wrapping it. When she was leaving, she was holding the bottle in her hand and while wearing her shoes, the bottle slipped, fell down and broke into numerous pieces big and small which nearly covered the entire floor of the room. She felt awful. She hurriedly wanted to pick up the glass pieces but my wife prevailed and sternly told her to stand still in one place (a big punishment for Neha) while my wife picked up the pieces. My wife didn't want Neha to move around and get hurt. After the job was done my wife gave Neha her shoes and asked her to leave. Poor Neha!! – must have felt very sad, but she got over it pretty soon.

All said and done, we look forward to Fridays and eagerly wait for her arrival. I think all Senior Citizens whose children have gone abroad should fill their void by inviting some close child/children once a week and give them a nice tasty meal and in return they will get immense happiness.

CHAPTER 12

AASANAS & PRANAYAM

When I was a child, I used to feel funny watching my grandfather lying down on a piece of cloth and twisting and turning his body in a weird manner. More funny was to hear his gasses come out loud and clear from both his ends. I used to wonder why he is doing all this!! I was totally oblivious of the ailments of old age.

As I grew up, from a child to a young man, my body kept gaining more and more strength. Good healthy food and regular visits to gymnasium made sure that my body remained strong and disease free. As years rolled on and I hit forty, I noticed that now I was on a downward curve as far as my health and strength was concerned. When I retired at the age of sixty, I was disease free but slightly low on my strength.

Years rolled on and as I added five more years to my life, I also added certain ailments to my body. My joints started aching, particularly the knee and the shoulders. I was doing regular exercises but I noticed that the body was gradually deteriorating. Nearing seventy, I found that I couldn't get up easily if I was sitting on the ground. Getting in and out of a car was becoming a very difficult proposition. On my friend's advice, I visited a homeopath. He gave me some pills. I was also told to eat multi vitamin and calcium tablets. But nothing seemed to work well and I kept losing strength.

An old man with whom I used to take my evening walks and speak about each other's ailments, said to me, "Why don't you try doing Yoga". There was a young lady who was a yoga teacher and who lived in the same society in which I was living. I went to her and she told me that she will come home and do the needful. She told me to get a mat on which to do the various aasanas. That's when I remembered my grandfather at whom I used to laugh during my childhood days. Now I had become a laughing stock to my grandchildren. They used to laugh and copy me and do the various aasanas with such ease while I had to struggle to do even the simple aasanas. But I noticed that the aasanas were doing good to me. My body, which was becoming more and more stiff with age, was becoming a little more flexible by doing the aasanas regularly.

The same teacher told me that she was also trained in Pranayam and that if I do it under her guidance, it will certainly do a lot of good to my body. She further said that "Our life depends on oxygen. If oxygen is denied to our body, the body will die. If proper amount of oxygen is supplied, the body will feel nice and healthy. Pranayam is an art of breathing which ensures that good amount of oxygen is given to the body".

I appreciated the logic behind Pranayam and decided to do it regularly. I must confess that after a session of aasanas and Pranayam which used to last for an hour and fifteen minutes, I used to feel energized and the various aches in the body also started reducing.

My advice to young and old – instead of taking pain killer tablets, which have side effects, join the Yoga classes and believe me, you will be much happier, healthier and feel more energetic.

45

CHAPTER 13

FIGHTER PILOT'S WIFE

God made females and males in all organisms and gave them the ability to reproduce to keep their species alive. He must be a super mathematician to ensure that the balance between the males and females is maintained even through many generations. God must also be a super engineer to have designed the body of each and every organism in such an intricate manner.

Male and female coming together is a natural process. Humans regularise this as marriage. This process of marriage is generally accomplished by humans in two ways – either as arranged marriage or as love marriage. It is difficult to say which way is better – both the ways have their advantages and disadvantages. In love marriage, there is no importance given to parents in deciding the partners. One fine day, the partners just surprise the parents by saying, "Meet my spouse". While in arranged marriage more importance is given to parents than to partners. After having checked all details of the mutual families and having come to an agreement, the parents call the partners saying, "Meet your spouse".

In case of a Fighter Pilot, it is mostly arranged marriage because the first love of a fighter pilot is flying and most don't have the time to go wooing the girls. In today's scenario the partners are given a chance to meet each other and their OK is taken before proceeding further. Let me give you an excellent example of an arranged marriage of a Fighter Pilot.

There was a Fighter Pilot – let's call him Joshi –Joe for short. Joe had put in 8 years of commendable service. He was commissioned as a fighter pilot at the age of 21 yrs. He was a top class Fighter Pilot. And then, there was a girl – let's call her Jayashree Naik – Jaya for short. Jaya had just finished her double graduation in Home Science. She was 24 years old and her parents were getting restless to get her married. They were looking for a suitable boy for last two years. Then one fine day someone told them that, "We know of a family named Joshi. They have a son who is a Fighter Pilot in the Indian Air Force. They are a nice family and the boy is smart. We feel that he will be a right choice for your daughter".

So the Naik family went to meet the Joshi family. Marriages are made in Heaven they say. The two families exchanged notes, queried about each other's family details – past and present, and finally it was decided to arrange a meeting between Joe and Jaya. The meeting was arranged in Naik family's home and after exchanging pleasantries, Joe and Jaya were asked to go up in the terrace and were given total privacy to ask each other whatever they wanted to.

At first sight Joe had liked Jaya and even Jaya had found him smart. Though Joe had liked Jaya, he wanted to brief her about the life in the Air Force so that before giving consent for the marriage she is fully aware of what is demanded from a fighter pilot's wife. So he said to her, "Listen Jaya, Fighter Pilot's life is indeed dangerous and that is why I am telling you about the dangers involved in a fighter pilot's life. You need not give your consent for marriage right away. I would like you to think over and then say Yes or No. You are a beautiful girl and I am sure that you will get a very "well to do" boy earning decent amount of money and leading a very safe, stable life.

One other thing which I want to tell you is that a Fighter Pilot moves from place to place on posting in every 2 to 3 years. Service demands this of him. Having obtained proficiency on one type of fighter aircraft, he has to move to some other Squadron positioned elsewhere to get proficiency on another type of aircraft. So if you marry me, you may not have a stable life. You will have to get used to this and more than you, our children will have to get used to it. Whereas if you marry a civilian you will have a much stable life and so will your children.

Yet another thing that I want to tell you is that you may have to stay in remote places where you may not get an opportunity to do any job. You are a very qualified girl and you may feel frustrated for not being able to use your education. Think of all this, discuss with your parents and your friends and when you arrive at a well-considered decision, let me know. Even if your decision is a NO, I am ready to accept that and we shall part ways without any hard feelings. Bye, Take care and have no pressure while taking your decision".

Jaya had given a deep thought to what Joe had said. She herself was inclined to take up the challenge and marry Joe but nevertheless, she also consulted her parents and friends. They all had given her a positive advice and had said to her, "Jaya, you are really lucky to have an Air Force boy proposing to you for marriage and that too a Fighter Pilot.

He is ready to take risks and put his life at stake to serve our country. Isn't that commendable? We think you should admire him for that. Marrying a Fighter Pilot also amounts to taking a risk but we think it is also your duty to share this risk with him". So said, the mind was made up and the decision was conveyed to Joshi family. Marriage was held shortly and both lived happily for years.

CHAPTER 14

KENDRIYA VIDYALAY

Most of the children born to civilian families get to study in one place and in one school. Many of them spend nearly ten to twelve years in the same town, in the same environment, in the same school, under the same teachers and with same friends. As opposed to this, children of the Air Force (AF) Officers, who get posted out on an average of every two years, keep changing their school. They get an opportunity to see different places, go to different schools, make different friends and enjoy different atmosphere. For such children Central Schools (Kendriya Vidyalayas – KV for short) have been created.

Let us take an example of one KV and see its pros and cons. Two children of an AF officer – let's call them Dilip and Diya, studied right from first standard to twelfth standard in various KVs. Dilip got admitted in first standard in KV Halwara located in Punjab. Two years later their father was posted to AF Stn Tambaram located near town Chennai (earlier name Madras). That's when Diya got admitted in first standard in KV Tambaram. Dilip too was given admission in same KV in third standard. Both Dilip and Diya had their further education in various AF Stations where their father was posted on an average of every two years. They got a chance to study in various KVs located in different States like Bengal, MP, Maharashtra, Punjab etc.

In all KVs, students had to study the local language as one of their subjects and that is how both Dilip and Diya got to learn and speak in many languages. They often used to fight in local language!! – a great plus point of studying in KVs.

Initially Dilip and Diya found it a bit difficult to go from one KV to another. But they soon got used to it so much so that they used to eagerly look forward to their father's posting to another place. Going from one KV to another wasn't much of a problem because the books didn't change, uniform was same and the subjects and syllabus too was same.

Another plus point of studying in KV was that there was no differentiation in giving admission to children of officers, children of technicians who were not officers and children of lascars who were classified as class IV personnel. So all children were treated the same way irrespective of which class their parents belonged to. So, son of a lascar got to mix with son of an officer at the same level without any inferiority complex and so did the son of an officer had no superiority complex. As against this, students in private schools generally got to study only with children of rich parents.

Yet another plus point of KVs was their Fee structure. As compared to Private schools, the fee structure of KV's was very low and made affordable to all class of parents and that is how the children of poor class of parents could study with children of officer class.

CHAPTER 15

DISASTER MANAGEMENT

The recent heavy rains in India causing devastating floods once again highlighted the urgent need for us to put in place a well-considered Disaster Management Scheme. In India, are we prepared for various calamities like earth quakes, floods, uncontrolled spread of diseases etc? Or do we wait for the disaster to occur and then try and salvage the damage in whatever way we can, like mostly calling the Defence Forces for help?

Well, let us first understand certain fundamentals. There is something that we call as a disaster and there is something called as a hazard. A hazard is a phenomenon like a cyclone, earthquake, fire, flood etc. A hazard becomes a disaster when death and destruction result from such a hazard. If a cyclone passes over the sea where there is no habitation, we do not call it a disaster. Similarly if an earthquake occurs and there is no damage or destruction or deaths, it is not classified as a disaster.

Some say that most of the disasters are manmade. If we know that earthquakes do take place in certain areas and yet we do not construct quakeproof buildings there, then naturally we are asking for trouble. Knowing fully well that flooding takes place regularly in certain areas and yet we make buildings in such low lying areas, then we are naturally converting hazards into disasters. Disasters can be classified into two categories – natural and manmade. Natural disasters are cyclones, floods, draughts, earthquakes, landslides, volcanic eruptions, forest fires etc. While manmade disasters are accidents, epidemics or uncontrolled spread of diseases, gas leaks, NBC (Nuclear, Biological and Chemical) related situations etc.

It is felt that in most disaster cases, our approach to them is reactive rather than proactive. By reactive approach, it is meant that we start thinking of tackling the event after it has occurred. We don't prepare for it in advance and stock up certain essentials that may be required once the event occurs. Our attitude is that first let the earthquake take place or let the cyclone come and cause damage, only then money will be released from the Disaster Contingency fund. Whereas the money should be given in advance so that necessary preparations can be made to face the disaster and reduce the extent of damage. It is necessary to have a proactive approach and create what are called as bricks (stocks) of commonly required items during disaster and store them.

In most disaster cases Defence Forces are called for salvaging the situation. Although the primary role of the armed forces is to defend the sovereignty of their country, their self-sufficient character and their capability to mobilize at short notice, enables them to play a significant role in disaster relief. In our country the armed forces though not trained, are invariably the first to reach the scene and provide succour. It however, needs to be remembered that they have their primary job to perform and hence must be relieved as soon as possible.

The creation of a quick reaction force by the State Govt which can be deployed immediately is very important. There is a need for the State Govt to educate the general public at the grass root level. Many do not know what to do, how to react and whom to contact when the disaster occurs. The State authorities must therefore implement some sort of a lecture programme at Panchayat level to educate the common man. What do you have to say?

CHAPTER 16

PEARLS OF WISDOM

Given below are some statements which I call as Pearls of Wisdom. I think they are applicable to all and particularly to those who are enjoying certain amount of Power and are occupying the top seat and are called Bosses. Generally most Bosses tend to think that they know everything and that they always take the right decision. They believe that they can do no wrong and hence do not entertain any opinion or advice from their subordinates. Following statements I think are worth reading and assimilating since they are applicable to all.

Generally a Boss thinks that most of his subordinates are shammers and want to avoid working as much as they can. He thinks that they must be supervised closely. That is not correct thinking. A Boss must remember that basically every individual likes to work provided he is given the opportunity and right environment. The Boss must therefore, ensure that the office environment is made comfortable and proper equipment is provided to every worker. Secondly, the Boss must have trust and faith in those working under him and more importantly he must make them feel that he has trust and faith in them.

He must believe in the fact that no one makes a mistake intentionally & deliberately. So, there is no point in getting angry. Most Bosses make this mistake. They suddenly lose their temper and start shouting at the individual who has made the mistake. Instead, the Boss must find the reason and the cause behind what has gone wrong with a cool head so that such a mistake is not repeated.

Time is a very valuable factor and a good Boss must respect his own time and the time of his subordinates as well. If he wants to call some subordinate to his office then he must give him a time and adhere to that time. Don't keep him waiting outside the office and waste his precious time. Remember that he also has a lot of work to do and time is as important to him as it is to you.

Another thing that some Bosses who suffer from verbal diarrhoea do, is to get into long winded talks. They get carried away by their own eloquence. They must ensure that their talk is crisp and to the point so that precious time is saved.

One of the Principles of good management states that a Boss, instead of taking all the credit himself for a good job done, must make his subordinates feel that the credit belongs to them. He must say to them, "Good job guys. This wouldn't have been possible without your sincere hard work". A statement like this coming from their Boss makes the subordinates happy and encourages them to perform better.

Another smart thing that a Boss must try and do is to manipulate the subordinates in such a way that when asked for their opinion, they give a decision which infact you as a Boss wanted to make. Let them feel proud of having taken a correct decision.

A Boss must try and keep the happiness level of his subordinates high. He should avoid being over critical. He must remember that a happy man works better. He must try to be humane. He must occasionally have a casual and light dialogue with his subordinates and try and find out whether they are happy on the home front or do they have any problem. If anybody has a problem, he should try and help him to get over the problem. And if you can solve his problem, he will be ever grateful and work for you better.

A Boss must try and be original. He should not try and imitate some other Boss whose style of functioning he likes because people will see through him. He must remember that he is being observed very closely by his subordinates. His every action and sentence is being monitored and interpreted and therefore he must be honest, straight and genuine. He must also try and be non-corrupt and impartial and more importantly ensure by his deeds that people perceive him as such.

Lastly a Boss must realise that his subordinates are paying respect to him just because presently he is their Boss. He should understand that this is a temporary phenomenon. The day he ceases to be their Boss, they will stop even looking at him and turn their eyes and attention to their next Boss. This reminds me of a story of a King and his Donkey. In good old days, when there were no vehicles, donkey was the main source of moving around. The King sitting on his decorated Donkey used to move around in his kingdom and all the citizens used to bow down and salute him. The Donkey thought that they all are saluting him. The day the King died, the Donkey noticed that no one is saluting him anymore. Moral of the story is that the Boss should not think like a donkey. He must understand that his subordinates are respecting his position and not him.

CHAPTER 17

IS THERE GOD?

A relation of mine who resides in the United States sent me a very thought provoking article on the subject of GOD. He is an atheist, I am not. I am more inclined to believing in the existence of GOD. The article was written by a scientist and scientists apparently believe only in those things that have adequate, perceivable, material proof. Obviously this gentleman was an atheist – where is the proof that GOD exists he questioned.

The article triggered me into thinking a little deeper in this subject. Many questions came to my mind like - Is GOD really there somewhere? If there is one where is he? Why can't I see him? People claim that they can see GOD when in a state of deep meditation? Can they really see him or are they imagining? What is this concept of RELIGION all about? Why so many religions? Why so many GODs? Can you have religion divorced from the concept of GOD? Can an atheist practice a religion? Is religion a philosophy or is it GOD oriented – and a host of other such questions overwhelmed me.

The author in his article has given reasons as to why people believe in the concept of GOD. I thought the reasons stated by him are logically very sound and cannot be refuted. I have tried to enumerate them in the succeeding paragraphs giving my views on them. The reader may of course have his or her own differing views

The author says that most of us are hard wired to believe in GOD. Talking scientifically and in modern language, it can be said that "Mind" is a consequence of the complex neuro-chemical structure of the human brain. The physical brain is said to be the hardware that operates on the software of consciousness that gets modified through memory-based experiences and habitual patterns which form the database. Right from birth a strong data base of belief in GOD is created which prevents any other thought process. I tend to agree with this. Most of us believe in GOD because our parents believe in GOD. We don't question his existence because we are brought up not to do so.

The other strong reason for believing in GOD is that most people are scared to disbelieve. "Fear of GOD" is put in them that should they disbelieve, GOD will get angry and some harm may come their way. And most don't want to argue with this logic or test it. Here again I agree with the author. Though some of us might waver in our belief in GOD, yet we don't want to question his existence because of this fear syndrome.

The most common reason I feel is that majority finds relief in this belief. If things go wrong, they pray to GOD and hand over the worries to him saying, "GOD is great. He will take care". Believing in certain rituals like taking a dip in holy Ganges on certain auspicious days at Hardwar, or a dip in the Sangam at Allahabad, or visiting Mecca Medina during Haj gives them moral courage to face the future with a make-believe feeling that having accomplished the ritual, nothing can thereafter go wrong.

The writer is of the opinion that majority of the people believe in GOD because they are scientifically quite illiterate and do not understand certain supernatural phenomenon. They feel it is the act of GOD like for instance certain supernatural cures to some chronic ailments. Lunar Eclipse is considered by them as an act wherein GOD has become angry and in general it is looked at as a bad omen and a bad period. Flood, Famine are considered as acts of GOD as a result of onset of "Kaliyug". I think this is true even today though literacy has picked up but I am amazed to note how even some of the literate gentry believes in these miraculous acts of GOD.

Then there are some who believe in the theory, "There must be some creator after all". How can things be there without a creator – they say. So if this earth exists with life on it and if this universe exits in such an orderly manner then there must be someone who has made it all to happen and who is controlling the strings – who else but GOD. I think it is quite a logical thought. Everything has to have a maker, a creator or can things just happen by themselves without anybody doing them?

Well, having read so far, what do YOU feel about the existence of GOD? As far as I am concerned, I am a believer in the concept of GOD but I don't care much whether he actually exists or not. I find no sense in debating this issue. The prime question in my opinion is not whether there is GOD or not, the prime question is how to seek and achieve that inner peace. People say that belief in GOD and in your religion is the easier path to attain this. I know for sure that I get lot of solace in reciting the various "Shlokas" and "Mantras". They help me to pass my time most peacefully. They help me to forget my worldly worries. They help me to concentrate. They reduce my tension and blood pressure. I like the philosophy in them. I like the various lessons that are conveyed in them. No matter whether it is Geeta, Bible or Koran, they are great medicines to calm the turmoil in the inner self.

Then there are people who find GOD as a nice idea to lean on in difficult times. Such people rarely think of GOD when things are honky dory. But the moment misfortune strikes them, their belief in GOD is awakened and they visit all possible temples. They suddenly want to lean on him for support during this bad period. I think quite a few belong to this category. Many think of GOD and request for his support when they are nervous. Quite a few seek his blessings when they are starting something new. It gives them mental strength, moral courage and self-confidence. Children are asked to pay respects to GOD before going for their exams. This act removes/reduces the tension created by fear of Exam.

SO, ask yourself whether you believe in GOD and if so then Why? And if not then Why not?

63

CHAPTER 18

SOME DISTURBING THOUGHTS

I am sure all of us have disturbing thoughts. The first thought which I find very disturbing relates to Modern Technology. It is really amazing to see technology progressing in leaps and bounds in all spheres of human life. While that may be fine, we need not get flabbergasted by various inventions. After all, a nation need not strive for all the technology available in the world today. It has to relate the technological developments to it's needs.

Today, technology is on the verge of producing test tube babies and in time to come may even place grown up babies in the market for sale. But does India need this kind of technology? As long as we still take great pleasure and pride in producing our babies the conventional way, I don't think production of test tube or even grown up babies should have anything other than academic interest for us. The female population in our country takes great pride in earning their motherhood the way Mother Nature has designed it for them. A lot of the female population of the West wants motherhood the easier way. They want children but they don't want to bear them for nine months – how sad!! Perhaps this fact has been a driver to production of test tube babies.

The second disturbing thought relates to God given ability to think. This ability has its own plus and minus points. The biggest minus point is to indulge in negative thinking and end up in a state of depression. The positive side of thinking has given birth to many inventions. Initially I always thought that the activity of thinking is a sole prerogative of the head. But later as I grew up I realised that the thought process of the head is often interfered with by the heart. Many a times the head thinks and decides to do something but the heart says something else. And when the conflict between the head and the heart remains unresolved, then the stomach comes in – what we generally refer to as the gut feeling. If one suddenly faces a threating situation, like say a dog suddenly barking and running towards you, you don't have time to do rational thinking to take a decision. That is when gut feeling as a reflex action comes in. In a split second, you either decide to run or fight using your walking stick.

Yet another disturbing thought that keeps nagging me is whether to do good to a person or will he take advantage of it and use it against me. Let me give you an example. My early morning tea was habitually enjoyed in the balcony along with a few biscuits (British style!). We had a fair number of monkeys in our colony. One of them used to come quite close and watch me enjoying my tea. Perhaps the expression on his face stimulated a friendly instinct within me and one fine day I decided to share a biscuit with him. The next day he was again there and I gave him one more biscuit. This carried on pretty regularly for a few days.

One day I ran out of biscuits and I had nothing to give him. He waited for a while and after running out of patience started advancing quite menacingly towards me. I got scared and ran inside and that's when it struck me how a privilege can become a right, how someone can take advantage of your generosity. Aren't there a lot of such monkeys amongst us humans!!

Yet another disturbing thought that keeps nagging me is about Marriage. I think Marriage is a MATKA. It's a gamble. And whether you gamble at an early age or later in life, it doesn't really matter. After all it is a gamble. Some like to delay it and some play the game early enough. Whether it is an arranged marriage or a love marriage, it still is a gamble involving high stakes. Marriage is indeed a happy occasion but that happiness is laced with a sense of worry. Particularly these days, parents are always worried about "How long will it last?" They pray to God and keep their fingers crossed.

Well, do you experience some such disturbing thoughts? How do you tackle them?

CHAPTER 19

GAYATRI MANTRA

Gayatri mantra has been bestowed the greatest importance in Vedic Dharma. This mantra has also been termed as Savitri and Ved-Mata, the mother of the Vedas. Reciting this Mantra atleast ten times early morning soon after getting up gives one a lot of peace of mind. Infact whenever one feels disturbed, if one recites this Mantra, one soon starts feeling normal.

The Mantra is as follows :-

"Om bhur bhuvah swah

Tat sa vitur varenyam

Bhargo devasya dheemahi

Dhiyo yo nah prachodayat"

The literal meaning of the mantra is :- O God! You are Omnipresent, Omnipotent and Almighty. You are all Light, You are all Knowledge and Bliss. You are Destroyer of fear, You are Creator of this Universe, You are the Greatest of all. We bow and meditate upon Your light. You guide our intellect in the right direction.

The mantra also has a great scientific import. The modern astrophysics and astronomy tell us that our Galaxy called Milky Way or Akash-Ganga contains approximately 100 thousand millions of stars. Each star is like our Sun having its own planet system. We know that the Moon moves round the Earth and the Earth moves round the Sun along with the Moon. All planets move round the Sun. Each of the above bodies revolves at its own axis as well. Our Sun along with its family takes one round of the galactic centre in 22.5 crore years. All galaxies including ours, are moving at a terrific velocity of 20,000 miles per second. Isn't it frightening?

Let us now see the scientific meaning of the mantra step by step:-
(A) OM BHUR BHUVAH SWAH :-

Bhur the earth, bhuvah the planets (solar family), swah the Galaxy. We observe that when an ordinary fan with a speed of 900 RPM (rotations per minute) moves, it makes noise. Then, one can imagine, what great noise would be created when the galaxies move with a speed of 20,000 miles per second. This is what this portion of the mantra explains that the sound produced due to the fast-moving earth, planets and galaxies is "Om". The sound was heard during meditation by Rishi Vishvamitra, who mentioned it to other colleagues. All of them, then unanimously decided to call this sound "Om" the name of God.

(B) TAT SAVITUR VARENYAM :-

Tat that is God, Savitur that is the Sun (star), Varenyam – are worthy of bowing or respect. Once the form of a person along with the name is known to us, we may locate the specific person. Vishvamitra suggested that we could know (realize) the unknowable formless God through the known factors, viz., sound Om and Light of Suns / Stars.

(C) BHARGO DEVASYA DHEEMAHI :-

Bhargo the light, Devasya of the deity, Dheemahi we should meditate. The rishi instructs us to meditate upon the available form (light of Suns) to discover the formless Creator (God). Also he wants us to do Japa (recitation) of the word Om. This is how the sage wants us to proceed, but there is a great problem to realize it, as the human mind is so shaky and restless that without the grace of the Supreme (Brahma) it cannot be controlled. Hence Vishvamitra suggests the way to pray Him as under:-

(D) DHIYO YO NAH PRACHODAYAT:

Dhiyo (intellect), Yo (who), Nah (we all), Prachodayat (guide to right Direction). O God! Deploy our intellect on the right path.

Full scientific interpretation of the Mantra:- The earth (bhur), the planets (bhuvah), and the galaxies (swah) are moving at a very great velocity, the sound produced is Om, (the name of formless God.) That God (tat), who manifests Himself in the form of light of suns (savitur) is worthy of bowing/respect (varenyam). We all, therefore, should meditate (dheemahi) upon the light (bhargo) of that deity (devasya) and also do chanting of Om. May He (yo) guide in right direction (prachodayat) our (nah) intellect dhiyo.

Try reciting this Gayatri Mantra atleast ten times soon after getting up. You will not regret it. Instead you will be surprised to realise how your rest of the day passes peacefully. Personally I do this and get total peace of mind. My level of anger also comes under control. Whenever I am idle I do the Jap (recitation) of this Mantra. I suggest you Google and search for Gayatri Mantra, click on it and select Gayatri Mantra sung by Anuradha Paudwal 108 times in a very melodious way. You will be surprised to see the effect it has on your mind.

CHAPTER 20

<u>Mr AND Mrs "X"</u>

This is a story of an old couple. Let's call them Mr and Mrs "X". It was their fortieth wedding anniversary which was being celebrated. The couple had to organize the celebrations themselves since their son and daughter were away and well settled beyond the seven seas. They received the e-cards from them which they saw when they opened their mail in the morning and wondered whether the cards had been pre-generated to be sent on this day! They were almost certain that the kids were actually not aware that today was their marriage anniversary and that too fortieth one or else they would have given a ring early morning. Computers had really impersonalised the precious relationships which the couple so dearly cherished!!!!!!

The discussion between the two about the celebrations with respect to their fortieth anniversary had started almost ten days back which invariably always ended in a verbal fight. She wanted to hold it in the nearby hotel lounge whereas he wanted to hold it in their backyard lawn. She wanted to call hundred family friends whereas he felt that it would be a better idea to call just ten real close acquaintances, give personal attention to each of them and enjoy in their company rather than going to the hotel and ending up saying just "Hello" and "Thanks for coming" to most of them.

They had known each other for last forty years and three more years prior to their marriage. It had all started very well as most of the courtships and marriages start. The words "Darling" "Sweet Heart" were used by both of them rather profusely. But as years passed by, one Darling was referred to as "Stupid Man" and the other Darling as "Stupid Woman". Some years later as their vocabulary improved and their tolerance level for each other dropped to near zero, they graduated to calling each other as "You rabid Bitch" and "You Son of a Bitch". But the years of co-existence had bound them so intensely that despite using the strongest abuses, they still didn't want to separate. Infact, neither could they live peacefully with each other nor could they dare to separate. Both were worried about losing the partner and the subsequent lonely life.

The woman was more vocal than the man. It was generally she who made the first instigating remark. The man often tried to ignore and showed as if he had not heard her. But she wouldn't let him enjoy his peace – "How dare he not hear me!!". She would invariably repeat what she had said and instigate the man to respond. The man would finally lose his patience and say something in response and that would be his waterloo.

The two actually didn't require any pretext to start a fight. The fact that they got up in the morning was good enough to start the fight. Infact Fighting had become their major pass time. This frequent howling and shouting served as a tonic for both of them. It would pump up some extra adrenaline in their system and make them feel more energetic. The woman was a compulsive blabber. She claimed that it helped to keep her blood pressure down. She wouldn't pause even for a second between her sentences and if she did, the husband would feel uneasy and throw some remark to get her started. One small remark from him would rejuvenate her to blabber for next ten minutes. But when it came to difference of opinion or an argument, the husband was not allowed to put through even a word and if he tried, she would raise her voice couple of decibels to overpower him. The man once jokingly told his friends during their evening get together that the only time he was allowed to open his mouth during their arguments was to yawn and everyone had a hearty laugh shaking their heads as if saying "me too".

There was a small garden near the cluster of high rise flats which had mushroomed few years back. The old couple lived in one such flat. Almost all the flats, 120 to be exact, were occupied by residents of all ages. The old man and the woman were happy in their flat. Every evening as a ritual, the old man would stroll to the garden to attend the unofficial gathering of the oldies.

The gathering would last for nearly two hours. This time was used for cracking jokes and having a dig at each other. At the end of the session, they all would go back to their respective flats happy and contended and thankful to

God for having given them one more evening to enjoy. Their group consisted of oldies with ages varying from sixty to even ninety plus. Each one had his own story. By and large their stories were quite similar, the main factor being wife shouting and dominating. Ladies were not allowed. All the members were not entirely healthy. In fact each one suffered from one ailment or the other and some with multiple health problems but they all had resigned to their problems and learnt to live with them. The meeting did give lot of joy and confidence to all of them in their dying years.

CHAPTER 21

<u>Mr AND Mrs "Y"</u>

This is another interesting story of an old couple. Let's call them Mr and Mrs "Y". Mr "Y" had lost his wife almost ten years back when he was 65 years old. She had died because of heart failure. He could somehow never pardon himself for her death. He thought he was responsible for her heart attack. She had complained of a mild pain in the chest. His response to her was that it must be a muscle pain and that she should rub that area with an ointment. Poor thing listened to him and slept never to get up again. She had passed off in her sleep and the autopsy confirmed that she had died of cardiac arrest. Mr "Y" was heartbroken and his heart could not be repaired ever again, not even by the passage of time which is supposed to be a great healer.

They had two sons who were not staying in the same town. Both were married and had their own children to look after. They had flown in on hearing the sudden demise of their mother, attended the funeral and back they went leaving the old man to fight with the gloom all alone. Both didn't invite him to come along and spend a few days with them. The old man knew the reason. Their wives were working ladies and didn't have enough time to look after their own kids. Obviously, they didn't want to take any additional responsibility. Old man quite understood that and didn't blame them for their behaviour.

Ten years had passed since he had lost his dear wife. He had spent all these years all alone and missed his wife each day. Once in a while his eyes would shed some tears when he was alone and remembered some happy moments spent with her. She was a very tender loving person and had given him more love and care than he had expected. It had really been a very long and happy relationship.

When all alone and lying in bed, Mr "Y" often remembered how he had spent the initial years of his life after marriage. How he had tolerated all her mistakes with great amount of patience. Mrs "Y" had been a very poor cook. No matter how hard she tried, she could never manage to make tasty food but yet he had tolerated her bad cooking by saying "Darling, the dish is really good. I have never eaten such a delicious dish before. Why don't you send the recipe to Star Plus which telecasts the cooking programme"? But as years passed, he wondered how his tolerance level had gone down. She cooked a dish for dinner. As usual it was awful and how he had reacted saying "You stupid so-and-so. Haven't you learnt how to cook in so many years?", and how she had reacted saying, "You so-and-so, go and eat grass all I care. Don't ever ask me to cook food here after". Such and other thoughts brought a smile on his face and he wondered how life changes with passing years.

After her demise, he lived a routine life from which he rarely deviated. Morning walk was followed by a simple breakfast consisting of a boiled egg, two toasts, glass of milk and a banana or an apple. He organized the breakfast himself. One maid used to come around 1000h. The old man used to finish his bath before that and be ready to open the door for the maid. She would do sweeping and swopping, cook some vegetable, dal and make four chapattis, two for lunch and two for dinner and leave by 1100h. Hardly a word was spoken between them. The old man used this time for reading the newspaper. After the maid left, he would go to the club house and play cards. Get back around 1pm for his lunch and then a short snooze for an hour or so.

Around 4 pm, the only son of the maid would come after finishing his college to get few things from the nearby market. The old man was sponsoring his education. He was paying his college fees and also giving him money to purchase his books. The boy was doing well in his studies and that gave the old man some pleasure. Evening was spent along with the other oldies cracking jokes and generally enjoying. He never failed to hear the eight-O-clock news with a peg of whisky in hand followed by his second drink along with dinner. He was counting years and eagerly waiting to join his wife wherever she was.

CHAPTER 22

CLIMATE CHANGE

A wise man has made a very profound statement conveying that if we tamper with Nature, then Nature will get angry and as a consequence we will have to face disasters like floods, earth quakes, famines etc. Uncontrolled growth of population also amounts to tampering with Nature because earth can cater for a certain number of population and no more. This is backed by Malthusian Theory which states that if population growth outpaces agricultural production then there will be too many people and not enough food. He has conveyed that if we don't control the population then nature will control the population by creating calamities like famine, epidemics, plague etc.

We are already facing the wrath of Nature because of our uncontrolled production of Carbon Dioxide (CO_2) in the form of rising temperatures and rising sea levels. Today, climate change has become one of the most vigorously debated topic on Earth. This has been termed as "Green House Effect"

The Green House Effect is the effect caused by increase in the quantity of certain gases like CO_2, Water Vapour and other trace gases like Hydrogen, Helium, Neon, Krypton and Xenon. These gases effectively 'trap' heat in the lower atmosphere and reradiate it downwards. Without natural greenhouse effect, the earth would be about 60°C cooler than it is today – impossible to live in. So, it can be said that Greenhouse Effect by itself is not bad. Infact it is necessary. Our concern is not with the fact that we have a greenhouse effect, but whether human activities are leading to an enhancement of the greenhouse effect by the emission of greenhouse gases through fossil fuel combustion and deforestation.

Other predicted effects of global warming include melting of the polar ice caps, flooding of coastlines, severe storms, changes in precipitation patterns, and widespread changes in the existing ecological balance.

Present Human activity has been increasing the concentration of greenhouse gases in the atmosphere. If we continue to burn coal, oil, and gas at the rate that we are doing, then we will end up with the percentage of greenhouse gases doubling or even tripling in the near future resulting in severe global warming and in raising the level of sea water.

Scientists are concerned that continued global warming will accelerate ozone destruction. Ozone layer is a layer which contains relatively high concentrations of ozone. It exists in the Upper layer of Atmosphere called Stratosphere. Stratosphere is approximately 10 km to 50 km above Earth. Ozone depletion gets worse when the stratosphere becomes colder. Because global warming traps heat in the troposphere, less heat reaches the stratosphere which then gets colder. In other words, global warming can make ozone depletion much worse.

Although the concentration of the ozone in the ozone layer is very small, it is vitally important to life because it absorbs biologically harmful ultraviolet (UV) radiation emitted from the Sun. This UV radiation can be harmful to the skin and is the main cause of sunburn. Excessive exposure can also cause genetic damage, resulting in problems such as skin cancer.

The first international effort to address the greenhouse effect was the Kyoto (Japan) Protocol in December 1997. The treaty was negotiated for years and finally came into effect around Jan 2009. More than 170 nations signed the treaty.

Critics of the Kyoto Protocol particularly US focused on the fact that the treaty has levied restrictions only on the developed nations of the world and not on developing countries like China, India, and Brazil. The developing countries argued that for development they need to produce more energy and hence the restrictions should not apply to them.

It looks like a Catch 22 situation. Let's hope and pray that things get sorted out and our future generations don't suffer because of our selfishness.

CHAPTER 23

DEMEANING OF DEFENCE FORCES

India was under British rule for long years and the citizens had to fight hard and sacrifice innumerable lives to throw them out and gain freedom. On getting independence, India opted to function under Democratic system where the elected members of both the houses – Rajya Sabha and Lok Sabha, assisted by the bureaucrats (advisors) consisting of IAS (Indian Administrative Service) officers enjoyed all the powers. The Defence Forces never got to enjoy any powers or any say in the governance of the nation. As years went by, the standing of the Armed Forces was systematically and gradually degraded. The protocol was amended time and again and the status of the three Chiefs was lowered.

When an issue came up concerning procurement of equipment or change in policy concerning defence matters, the Chiefs could not take independent decisions. They had to refer the issue to Defence Secretary, Ministry of Defence (MoD) who pushed the file down and a parallel file was created. The matter was considered on this MoD file and finally the reply was sent signed by the Joint Director (equivalent to Brigadier) level to the letter sent by the Chief under his own signature addressed to the Defence Secretary. This was indeed demeaning. The Defence Secretary should have had the decency to adhere to the protocol and sign and send the reply to the Chief himself.

If one had to state an example of an Organisation which was enjoying absolute power without any attached responsibility, it was the Ministry of Defence. In the event of a war, should the war be lost, the blame would go to the Chiefs of the three Services. But the power to approve which equipment should be purchased to ensure operational preparedness remains with the Ministry, primarily the Defence Secretary. The Chiefs cannot spend even a single Rupee without the permission of the MoD officials.

If the Chiefs felt that certain equipment was urgently required else the operational status might get degraded, yet they could not buy it without going through the time consuming procedure of obtaining the MoD approval. The MoD officials had no technical knowledge about any weapon equipment. Most of them had never seen a tank or an aircraft or a ship. Quite a few officers had been posted to MoD from various Ministries like Health, Sports, Husbandry etc. For Defence Officers to deal with them was extremely frustrating and a test of patience, because lack of knowledge resulted in enormous delay in approval of the procurement of that equipment.

The MoD also held a tight control on promotions of officers above the rank of Colonels / Group Captains. Though the Defence Forces held Promotion Boards very meticulously, they could not promote the officers without the MoD sanctioning the Board.

For the last so many years the bureaucrats of the Defence Ministry and the Various Defence Ministers have given lip service and made false promises to the issues raised by the Defence HQs. Classic examples are the recommendations made by the Group of Ministers (GoM) after the Kargil debacle. Some of these still remain unfulfilled

Following the submission of the Kargil Review Committee (KRC) report, the PM set up a Group of Ministers to review the national security system in its entirety and in particular, to consider the recommendations of the KRC and formulate specific proposals for implementations. Some of the important recommendations made by GoM on which action is still pending are summarised below.

First important recommendation was regarding the functioning of the Chiefs of Staff Committee (COSC). The senior most Chief amongst the three Services namely Army, Navy and Air Force functioned as the President of COSC. He was the contact point between the Defence Minister and the Armed Forces. The recommendation quoted that the functioning of the COSC has revealed serious weaknesses and the Government needs to appoint a 5 star officer as "Chief of Defence Staff" (CDS) to function as a "Principal Military Advisor" to the RM. Finally after nearly 20 years, the present PM announced in his Independence Day speech on 15 August 2019 that he will create a CDS. But many want to take this with a pinch of salt because they wonder what status he will be given. Will he be placed above Defence Secretary or at par with him?

The apprehensions of the Defence Forces have turned true. Though CDS has been appointed, his status has been considerably diluted as compared to the recommendation of the KRC. Instead of a five star officer, a four star officer has been appointed as CDS with no major enhancement in power as compared to the Chairman COSC. Most in the Armed Forces are feeling cheated.

Next recommendation was that given the size of the country's defence apparatus and its substantial budget, there is a need to progressively decentralize decision making and delegate financial and administrative powers to the service HQs wherever feasible. The recommendation has still not been executed despite so many years gone by since Kargil war.

The committee also recommended that there should be amalgamation between the MoD and Defence Forces meaning that there should be inter posting of officers between the MoD and Defence Head Quarters. The issue is still pending because the bureaucrats are worried of losing their power.

Another flaw was with the announcing of the defence budget. It was invariably announced late but worst was that Forces could not spend all of allotted amount due to delayed approval of proposals on files by the MoD. The unspent money lapsed and was not shifted into next year's budget despite the Defence Forces crying hoarse to do so.

Because of this feeling of demeaning, Armed Forces personnel feel hurt. They don't want their children to join the Defence Forces. Once upon a time, joining Defence Force was the third best career option besides Doctor and Engineer. Today it has slid down to around 25th career option. Today if a young man is unable to join any other profession, he thinks of joining the Defence Forces. Today all three Services are functioning with deficient man power. Unless the Government gives a serious thought to this and takes some action, future of Defence Forces and consequently of the country will be bleak.

CHAPTER 24

USE OF THIRD DIMENSION

It is often forgotten that Air Force is comparatively a very young Service and has just about completed a century. In fact one of the first Air Forces, the Royal Air Force, was created in 1918. Army is perhaps as old as mankind and came into being ever since man started fighting on the ground in an organized manner. The Navy too is hundreds of years old and dates back to around the sixteenth century when economic interests clashed over the sea and battles were fought between the ships to establish dominance over blue waters. But young as it may be, the pace of advance in the field of aviation, since its inception in 1904, has been phenomenal because of the realization of the tremendous potential available in the use of the third dimension. This realization set about a fierce race amongst the leading nations for outsmarting and surprising the enemy with technological innovations.

As can be seen in the various wars and conflicts fought post WW-II, Air Power has played a very crucial and decisive role in most of them (for example Battle of Britain). No military action today, however, limited or localized in nature, (for example Kargil war), can be conducted without the involvement of Air Power.

With the induction of satellites, ballistic missiles and likely weaponisation of space in the near future, the term "Use of the Air" has been outdated and has been replaced by a more encompassing word namely "Aerospace Power", working definition of which can be said to be, "The ability of a nation to project military force by or from a platform in the third dimension above the surface of the earth". The third dimension includes outer space and the word Aerospace Power is now deemed to encompass the exploitation of space.

Besides the changes in technology, the nature and texture of threats have also undergone a gradual change. In good old days, threats mainly related to border invasion and capture of territory. Now, this is no longer true. Today, no country can invade an independent State and capture it with the intention of permanently holding it. The world opinion will simply not permit this sort of a thing to happen.

Many now feel that the future wars will be triggered by issues like shortage of water or oil. It is widely acclaimed that America invaded Iraq not because Iraq had weapons of mass destruction but because they wanted their oil. Many feel that future wars will mostly be Trade wars also called Economic Wars aimed at breaking the economy of the opponent.

Today's weapons are mostly controlled from Space, for example use of GPS (Global Positioning System) for guidance of these weapons. Communication is also mainly done through Space based satellites. So many experts feel that future wars will start for gaining dominance of Aerospace. The wars will therefore start with electronic warfare in an attempt to make the enemy blind. Net centricity will play a predominant role. Hacking enemy's net centric capability and damaging it will play a major role.

Other factors which will play an important role will be Gathering of Real time intelligence, Battle field surveillance, Post strike damage assessment, Functioning of IFF (Identification of Friend or Foe), GPS and Time synchronization which is very important for precision guidance of weapons.

India has many experienced software engineers with great hacking capability. They will make a great difference in the outcome of war. They will be our front line warriors. Just a thought – what do you have to say?

CHAPTER 25

DEFENCE FINANCE

In very simple words, Defence Finance has been defined as application of economic principles to defence related issues. Defence finance has always been a subject of great debate between the finance and defence people – defence people wanting more and more while the finance people wanting to give less and less – a debate between butter and guns as some call it. To put it very simply, this is so because defence personnel tend to think of defence detached from the overall economic health and development of the nation and finance people think of defence expenditure without relating it to operational requirements, threats and national security. Hence this tug of war.

Being a democracy with civilian rule having the upper hand, unlike in military ruled or autocratic States, in all probability Defence is likely to get a raw deal. Politicians and also the public at large often look at Defence as a wasteful expenditure giving preference and precedence to Diplomacy as a major weapon for dispute management. But the hard fact is that every Nation has to spend certain amount of precious money for creating a credible defence and the debatable question that arises is HOW MUCH?

National Security is a subset of Comprehensive National Power. Broadly, National Power can be said to consist of Economic Power, Conventional Power and Nuclear Deterrent Power. These are the three main constituents of National Power. The other lesser determinants are landmass, natural resources and population. A Nation State which has all the three main constituents in proper proportion can be considered as a Global Power. USA and Russia today fall into this category. China and India are aspiring to be included.

Normally when we talk of national security, we generally refer to it as border security that is provided by the Armed Forces. But is this concept of security valid today or has it changed? Some feel that today it is the economic security, energy security rather than border security that matters more. And they say that this Security depends on how strong the nation's economy is. They argue that the chances of having a conventional war where one nation attacks the other nation to gain territory to build subsequent bargaining power have greatly receded. Today the world is being controlled by market forces. So it is Money rather than Guns that determines the National security. They argue that it is perhaps time to have a paradigm shift in our concept of security. They feel that we need to shift to co-operative security concept. Alliances, Treaties, Assurances and Conventions can be means of ensuring low cost security. But those who oppose this thought process, feel that no matter how strong a nation becomes monetarily, it will always need to spend and develop matching conventional and nuclear deterrent to cater for unforeseen contingencies and they say that history is replete with examples where a militarily weak nation has been dominated by the stronger one.

Therefore, the question that arises is that "Is spending on defence total waste of precious resources? Is defence spending cost effective way of negotiating threats?" Well, some feel that it is cost effective. They say that the costs involved in conducting a war are so huge that it is perhaps more cost effective to spend on credible defence to avoid a war – a debatable thought but nevertheless has some merit. Wars devastate the economy of a country and put it back around 10 to 15 years so it is perhaps cost effective to spend enough on defence on a regular basis and create a kind of credible deterrence which will help avoid wars. They operate on the philosophy that if war has to be deterred then make it appear like an exorbitantly unaffordable affair to the adversary.

Yet another argument put forth by some in favour of spending on defence is that credible defence stimulates economic growth. They believe that good defence capability with safe internal security will invite foreign investment, tourism etc and thus help in improving the economy of the nation.

There are some people who feel that Globalisation, meaning economic integration and regional economic groupings, has reduced the possibility of war. On the contrary there are some people who feel that Globalisation provides for a new form of hegemonic domination by the developed over the developing.

Well, having read so far what is your Opinion on following thought provoking questions :-

1. Do you think that spending on Defence is a burden on National Economy?
2. Do you think that India should reduce its Defence Budget and use the saved money on developing its National Economy?
3. Do you feel that we need to shift to co-operative security concept like forming Alliances and Treaties which can be more cost effective way of ensuring security?
4. Or do you think that spending on Defence indirectly promotes foreign investment adding to National Economy?

Give it a good thought because it is a serious matter.

CHAPTER 26

HORSE SENSE

"Have some sense damn it"; "Fellow seems to have no sense at all"; "What a senseless thing to do!" – often heard sentences. What is this SENSE after all? One is normally aware of the five senses which a human body has like the sense of smell, sight, taste, hearing and touch. One has also probably heard of what is called as the "sixth sense". But the sense referred to in the above sentences is apparently quite different. Dictionary defines sense as faculty of perception; feeling; understanding; practical wisdom etc. There are many ways in which the word SENSE is used – "He has now come to his senses"; "There is no sense in worrying about the past"; "In a way, his talk doesn't make any sense!"; "Sense of Humour"; "Dress sense" and the like.

I would like to define SENSE as the ability to do something quite naturally and quite right. You must have heard people saying that so and so has road sense. Such a person is perhaps not likely to have an accident on the road. But then there are some irritating people who do not have road sense at all and are very likely to have some sort of accidents on the road.

You need to have sense to cook well, you need sense to decide when to talk and what to talk and when to keep shut. You need to have sense to bowl well to become a good bowler. As a matter of fact you need sense to do anything well and right. A sensible man will generally do everything well. Can it be called as common sense? I don't think so, I think it is something else. Can it be developed? Yes, I think it can.

Let me tell you a story about a NDA (National Defence Academy) coursemate of mine who had no horse sense at all. In fact he had no sense about anything at all when he joined NDA. It did not take very long for his course mates to nick name him as "Sloppy". Sloppy was mortally scared of horse riding. Apparently he had no "horse sense" at all. The horse in fact had more sense than him to determine what kind of rider was sitting on its back and didn't lose much time to buck if it found that a senseless rider was sitting on top.

Cadets had to go for riding once in a fortnight. Sloppy could never sleep the previous night. Whole night he would keep awake imagining and dreading the awful fall that he would have the next day. He used to save the morning biscuits that the cadets were given with their morning tea for the horse. He used to religiously bribe the horse with those biscuits before the riding lesson started hoping that the horse would show some mercy towards him.

In the riding school, cadets used to be divided into what was called as "Rides". Each Ride had about eight cadets. After the initial fall-in, the Rides used to be marched to where the horses were lined up. Eight cadets used to be lined up opposite the eight horses and one generally had to take the horse which was standing directly in the front. If one was lucky, one got a docile horse, if not, one had to ride a frisky horse.

Sloppy somehow always got a frisky jumpy horse who looked all set to throw him off the moment Sloppy mounted it. Horses are indeed intelligent creatures. They can easily distinguish a good rider from a bad one. They can even sense the confidence level of a rider. Poor Sloppy! – he almost always fell off, not just once but a number of times during those two hours of riding period. The moment the Ride used to start the trot, Sloppy would invariably go out of sync with the horse and was seen slowly rolling to one side and then bending forward and hanging on to the neck of the horse as if wanting to embrace it. Apparently, all the horses hated such frequent display of affection and they used to buck in no time and off used to go Sloppy.

But as time passed, Sloppy developed horse sense. He developed adequate confidence to eat the biscuits himself instead of sparing them to bribe the horse. It is a treat to see the well looked after NDA horses. They are amazingly well trained. When the "Sahab" (the riding instructor) ordered a left turn all the horses would turn instantaneously and if the rider wasn't prepared, the centrifugal force would get the better of the rider throwing him off outwards. Sloppy with his improved horse sense managed to counter that centrifugal force after having had innumerable falls.

The riding school had jumping tracks, some straight and some round. When the horse was brought on the start line, it would take off and start jumping whether the novice rider willed it or not. It would jump away to glory without bothering whether the rider was still on top or left behind. At times some horses would suddenly stop at a jump and the momentum of the rider, who had a loose grip of the horse, would take the rider across the jump. Initially Sloppy was terribly scared of this activity but as time passed, Sloppy developed the sense to feel as a part of the horse and started enjoying all aspects of horse riding so much so that he later took part in exhibition jumping.

CHAPTER 27

HOW DOES A FIGHTER PILOT THINKS?

There are many phases in fighter flying which do not give a fighter pilot the liberty of thinking logically before deciding on what action to take. Many a times he has to act instantaneously, either instinctively or intuitively. Instantaneously means immediately without any wastage of time. Instinctively means without conscious thought. Such actions are not planned or developed by training. They are based on instinct and not on thought analysis. Instinctively can also be defined as automatically, involuntarily, spontaneously, unconsciously, inadvertently, a sort of a reflex action. An example could be a split second decision to eject (meaning get out of the misbehaving aircraft) initiated by survival instinct. Intuitively means by using ones feelings rather than by considering the facts – what some people call as gut feeling. If in a war involving group aerial combat to shoot down the enemy aircraft, the thought process in the mind of a fighter pilot would be a classic combination of logical, intuitive and instinctive thinking with perhaps intuitive thinking having a major share.

The probability of correctness of the action taken after logical thought process is expected to be quite high as compared to the action taken Intuitively or Instinctively and instantly. In a fighter pilots profession of flying, where he does not get adequate time to resort to logical thinking and has to act intuitively on several occasions, the possibility of making mistakes can be quite high. Let us give a little deeper thought to the way the mind works and see if the probability of making mistakes while taking intuitive actions can be reduced.

In an article written by VV Rampal in Times of India in the column "The Speaking Tree", he has talked of the mind having two modes of functioning – one through reasoning and other through intuitive thinking. He says that reasoning mind is a consequence of the complex neuro-chemical structure of the human brain. Brain is divided into two halves. It is said that the right half deals with intuitive thinking while the left half does logical thinking.

The two modes of thinking namely one through reasoning and the other through intuitive thinking operate at two different levels. One analyses external experience and the other has inner vision. It is believed that human senses generate the data and then based on this data, one takes a decision through conscious reasoning. The physical brain is said to be the hardware that operates on the software of consciousness that gets modified through memory-based experiences and habitual patterns which form the database – so says VV Rampal.

Can one precondition one's mind to act intuitively in a certain way in certain situations to ensure less mistakes? Well, the answer I feel is yes. A pilot must be aware of what are known as "Act" emergencies. These are the emergencies in which one is not expected to think and then act – one is expected to just act spontaneously. An example can be Engine failure in a single engine aircraft soon after take-off. In such a case there will be no time to think and then act. The pilot must act based on the action laid down for this kind of "ACT" emergency. In this case the laid down action could be to "EJECT".

In his spare time, a pilot must think many times of the various ACT emergencies and the relevant actions to be taken. He must simulate them in training simulators number of times so that instantaneously he takes the correct action intuitively. I would like to believe that this intuitive action can be refined by pre-thinking of various situations and creating a databank in your brain of various correct actions that ought to be taken. That is where experience counts. An experienced pilot will intuitively act more correctly than one with less experience because his database is strong.

CHAPTER 28

THE ART OF MANAGEMENT

The word Management is a very versatile word and can be used in many ways for example like managing one's expenditure, managing one's subordinates, managing one's health, managing one's family (spouse and children) etc.

It is a noun as well as a verb. As a noun it is defined as the process of dealing with or controlling things or people. As a verb it can be said that the situation was managed well. Dictionary meaning of management is, "Management is a set of principles relating to the functions of planning, organising, directing and controlling. It is application of these principles in harnessing physical, financial, human and informational resources efficiently and effectively to achieve organisational goals".

Let us discuss management of a small company by a Boss. Let us presume that he has ten subordinates in his company. The first thing he should do is to "Organise" his company. He must appoint a No 2 to himself. He should then make it clear to the rest that "X" is my No 2 and he will take over all responsibility from me in my absence. He should also tell everyone to consider that instructions coming from him are in fact coming from me. You will be surprised how happy and motivated Mr "X" will feel. His dedication and loyalty towards you will simply shoot up.

The next thing that the Boss must do is to lay down a protocol and make a tree describing the structure of the company. If there are two architects, nominate who is senior amongst the two. Make it clear to them that the senior architect will be held responsible should anything go wrong in designing the architecture. And also make it clear that the senior architect will deal with him through Mr "X" and that he should consider Mr "X" as his primary Boss. This can be termed as Organising your personnel as shown below :-

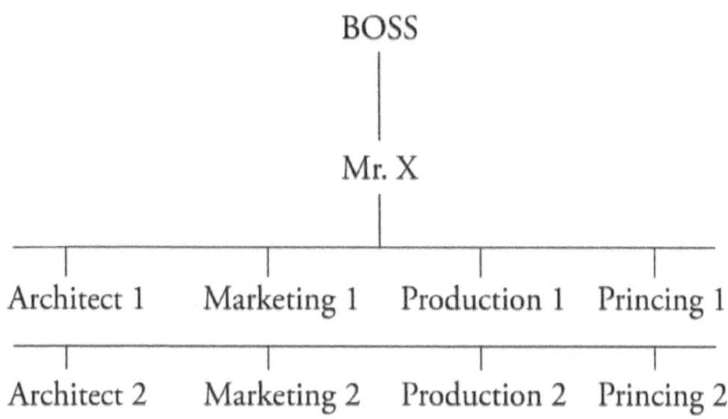

It should also be made clear that Annual Performance Report (APR) of everyone will be raised end December of each year by the immediate superior meaning APR of Architect 2 will be made by Architect 1. This report will be sent to Mr "X" and after writing his remarks, it will be sent to the Boss. Same procedure will be followed by other Departments. The APR of Architect 1 will be raised by Mr "X" and sent to the Boss. The APR of Mr "X" will be raised by the Boss himself. It should be made clear to everyone that the Boss retains the right to fire anyone whose annual performance is not up to the mark by giving him one month notice.

The next thing that a Boss must do is to create good working atmosphere in the office. He must give every subordinate an enclosure and make him feel that it is his office and he is the Boss in that space. Just to make him feel so, he must knock on his door and request for permission to come in. A small action like this will do wonders in making that subordinate feel important. Boss must remember that every worker wants to work sincerely and wants to give his best provided he is given the right environment. He must equip the offices of all his subordinates with proper table, chair, stationary, computer and even a table fan if required to make them feel comfortable.

Another important thing that the Boss must do is to give complete freedom to the subordinates to work and not sit on their head. He must ofcourse direct them but not supervise them to the extent that they lose their initiative. Having given broad directions, he must give them liberty to work as they wish. He must trust that they will perform as directed and more importantly make them feel that they are enjoying his complete trust.

Once in a while, he must visit their offices not with the intension of finding faults but to praise them by saying something like, "Oh, you are doing a great job. Keep it up. I am sure that you will meet the deadline". In case he happens to notice that a particular subordinate is going the wrong way then instead of getting angry and shouting at him, he must control himself and correct him by saying, "Instead of what you are doing, why don't you try doing this. It might give you better result". In this way, the ego of the subordinate will not be hurt and he will be grateful to the Boss for his timely guidance.

I feel that Management is more of an art than science. Scientifically one can lay down Rules of Management but finally it is the art of using these rules. What do you feel?

CHAPTER 29

RELIGIOUS CHAOS

It is strange to notice how many Religions and Sub-Religions we humans have created. Besides the fights between two different Religions, it is also strange to get to know the kind of infighting that goes on within a Religion. If we look back we will notice that any Religion is created to gain Power and to amass followers. A sub-religion gets created once again with the same intention when there is severe disagreement between two proponents. An American writer has written some astonishing facts about various Religions.

Let us consider Muslim Religion. It was originated by Prophet Muhammad who died in AD 632. The succession to Muhammad became the central issue that split the Muslim community into several divisions most prominent amongst them being Shia and Sunni branches of Islam.

One of the biggest differences between Shia and Sunni Muslims is the importance that the Shiites give to Ali whom the Sunni do not recognise as being the prophet's rightful successor. Ali was the cousin and son-in-law of Muhammad who was regarded as the rightful immediate successor to Muhammad as an Imam by Shia Muslims.

Sunnis believe that Mohammad had no rightful heir and that a religious leader ought to be elected through a vote amongst the Islamic community people. They believe that Muhammad's followers chose Abu Bakr who was a close friend and advisor to Muhammad as his successor.

There are about 13 castes amongst Muslims. It is surprising to note that a Shia Muslim will not go to Sunni mosque and vice a versa. These two will not go to Ahamadiya mosque (a Muslim branch founded by Mirza Ghulam Ahmad). These three will not go to Sufi mosque. (Sufism is the mystical branch of Islam. It emphasises the inward search for God and shuns materialism). These four will not go to Mujahiddin mosque (The term Mujahideen refers to spiritual muslim warriors. The sect was created in 1829). One Allah, one Quran and one Nabi (Prophet) and yet such chaos!!

Now let's turn to Christianity. Bible is the authority for Christian faith. Christianity is the religion that is based on the birth, life, death, resurrection and teachings of Jesus Christ. Christianity began in the first century AD after Jesus died as a Jewish sect.

The religion had schisms and theological disputes that resulted in four main branches. The Roman Catholic church, the Eastern Orthodox churches, Oriental Orthodoxy and Protestant churches. It is amazing to know that a Latin Catholic will not enter a Syrian Catholic church. These two will not enter the Marthoma church. These three will not enter the Pennthacost church. These four will not enter the Salvation Army church and it goes on. You will be surprised to know that there are 146 castes of Christianity in Kerala alone and they will never share their churches. One Christ, One Bible and One Jehovah (Another name for God) and yet what chaos!!

Now let us talk about the Hindu Religion. It will amaze you to know that for this Religion there exist something like 1200 books and scriptures, about 10,000 commentaries and 1 lakh sub-commentaries. Hindu Religion has about 33 million Gods, thousands of Rishies, over hundred languages and yet no infighting. Everyone is allowed to visit any temple that he chooses to. Don't you find that very surprising??

CHAPTER 30

LAUGHTER-THE BEST MEDICINE

Have you ever visited a cancer patient in a hospital? Have you noticed the morose expression on his face as if he is going to die shortly? If you visit him with an expression indicating that probably you will not be able to see him again, then your visit will lower his morale further. But if you enter his room with a nice smile and crack a nice pre-planned joke based on your earlier association with each other, it will make him laugh and you will see his face light up. That is the magic of laughter.

I have gone through this myself. I was hospitalised because I got cancer. Lot of people came to see me with consoling expression. They thought that they are having a last look at me and that I would shortly dia. I used to hate their sad expression. It would make me sadder. So instead of bucking me up, I had to buck them up by telling a joke!! I had memorised some jokes for such people. I used to feel happy to see them go back home with a smile on their face and with a feeling that I am not going to die after all.

Well, I strongly believe that laughter is a great medicine. There was a park near our flat. Every morning I used to see bunch of old people gather in a group and laugh very loudly. Initially I thought that they are going crazy. But when I learnt about this Laughter Therapy, I started practising it and it did a lot of good to me. I started feeling more energetic and positive.

So friends, I have got some short jokes here which will light up your face and make you feel happy. Try remembering them and use them to make people laugh.

- A Chinese couple Mr & Miss Hua got twins without marriage.

What did they name them?

They named them as 'Jo-Hua', 'So-Hua'

- Santa: People consider me as a "GOD"
Banta: How do you know??
Santa: When I went to the Park today, everybody said, Oh GOD! U have come again.

- Banta Singh happened to be in a queue at a railway station ticket counter with two men ahead of him.

'Ek Punjab Mail dena.' demanded the man in front. He was given a ticket.

'Ek Punjab Mail dena.' the second man asked and was handed a ticket.

Then came the turn of Banta Singh, 'Ek Punjab female dena'

'What do u mean by Punjab female?' asked the clerk.

'It is for my wife' replied Banta Singh.

* Man: Is there any way for long life?
  Dr: Get married.
  Man: Will it help?
  Dr: No, but the thought of long life will never come.

* Prospective husband: Do you have a book called "Man, The Master of Women"?
  Salesgirl: The fiction department is on the other side, sir.

* Sardar was busy removing a wheel from his auto.
  > A man asks sardar why are you removing a wheel from your auto.
  >sardar : Can't you read the board. Parking is only for 2 wheeler.

* On a romantic day sardar's girlfriend asks him.
  Darling on our engagement day will you give me a ring.
  >Sardar: Ya sure, from landline or mobile.

So, have these jokes brought a smile on your face – I am sure they have. Have they raised your morale – I am sure they must have. Are you feeling better and happier? Such jokes also help to release your tension. So arm yourself with more such jokes and use them as frequently as you can. God Bless.

CHAPTER 31

TEACHINGS OF THE GEETA

Basically Geeta is a song sung by lord Krishna to inspire Arjun to fight. It has 18 chapters and a total of 700 verses. It is full of practical advice which is very much applicable to all of us even today to live happily in the world. What follows is an abridged form of some of the important teachings contained in these verses.

When Arjuna saw some kith and kin in the enemy army of Kaurawas, Arjuna suddenly lost his nerve saying, "How can I kill my near and dear ones?"

Lord Krishna urged Arjun to fight for his rights. He reminded him that as a warrior, it was his duty to fight in the declared war and establish peace, law and order in the world.

When Arjun still refused to fight, lord Krishna explained to him the meaning of death. He said to him that by killing his near and dear ones, all that he is doing is to release them from the bondage of their bodies. When you kill them, their Body will die but their Soul (Atma) will remain alive. Soul is energy and nothing can kill Atma. As explained in Science – "Energy in this universe is constant. It can neither be created nor destroyed. It can only be changed from one form into another". Whoever thinks that when a person dies both body and soul die, has not understood the nature of soul. Soul does not kill anyone and cannot get killed by anyone.

Lord Krishna further elaborated saying, "Arjun, if you still feel that Atma too dies along with the Body, then remember that whoever or whatever takes birth must die one day and whoever dies must be born again. This is the Law of Nature so why lament death".

Another advice given by lord Krishna to Arjun and applicable to all of us is, "Don't think of the result while executing some work. Your job is to concentrate and do your best in performing that job. Put all your attention and energy into every minute of performance of the job. Because if you keep thinking of the result then you will not be able to put your heart and soul in performing that job and the outcome may suffer. Do your best at the present moment and let the future take care of itself".

During the discourse of Geeta, Krishna has also explained the various ways to reach God. The most recommended way to seek God is through "Karma Yoga". This is the path of selfless service. Followers of this path do not have to leave work and go to an Ashram. They do all work for the greater good of society even by neglecting personal gain. With a little effort even a common ordinary human being can follow this path of Karma Yoga for attaining "Moksha or Nirvana – freedom from rebirth".

The second way to seek God is through the path of Spiritual Knowledge. Followers of this path go to a spiritual master or a Guru in an Ashram and under his able guidance they study the various Vedic scriptures hoping to seek God.

The third path is called the path of meditation. It is a path to develop control over your mind, senses and desires. One who can attain control over his mind is said to be united with God. The simple method of meditation uses the technique of reciting the word "OM".

Geeta has been recognised as the best scripture by many. Personally, I would recommend everyone to not just read it but understand it. I am sure that it will have a good effect on your blood pressure and mental health.

CHAPTER 32

THERAPIES IN MEDICINES

I am not a doctor but as a common man who is subject to various ailments and discomforts, I decided that I must know something about treatment of these common ailments. I think that it is very important to get full medical done regularly every year specially after crossing 60 years of age. It must be a comprehensive test including blood test for sugar, urine test, BP, X-ray of chest, ECG and also ultra sound of liver, kidneys and stomach area. Also, if at any time you suspect that some organ is not functioning properly, then without wasting time, you must visit a Doctor and get yourself checked. Remember that unnecessary delay can be fatal.

I think we humans are the only creatures who enjoy the services of Doctors. I don't think any other organisms have doctors. I think they all believe in letting the body cure itself. I was surprised to know that there are nearly thirty different types of doctors amongst us humans. There is a specific type of doctor for almost every major system located in the human body like Cardiologists, Gynaecologists, Dentists, Neurologists, Oncologists, Paediatrician and a host of others. We are lucky that medical science has progressed so much which has resulted in our longevity going up.

Out of curiosity I decided to find out what therapy and logic is being used by various medical sciences to cure the various ailments. Today, many people talk of Homeopathy being better than Allopathy. Some even talk in favour of Biochemic Salts. And some even talk of Bach Flower Treatment. So I decided to find the logic behind each type of treatment.

<u>Allopathy</u> refers to use of medication to treat or supress symptoms or the ill effects of the disease. It is based on the belief that disease is caused by imbalance among the four "humours" - blood, phlegm, yellow bile and black bile. These were in turn associated with the fundamental elements of air, water, earth and fire from which our body is supposed to have been made. Allopathy aims at treating the disease symptoms rather than treating their underlying causes. For example, if a patient has headache, then allopathy medicines will remove the headache and not the "cause" which is responsible for the headache. Also, most of the allopathic medicines have side effect.

<u>Homeopathy</u> as opposed to Allopathy, aims at removing the "Cause" of the ailment rather than the symptoms. It is a system of alternative medicine created in 1796 by a German Physicist named Samuel Hahnemann. Based on his doctrine of "like cures like", a claim was made by him that a substance that causes the symptoms of a disease when it is administered in healthy people, then the same substance would cure similar symptoms in sick people. Though slow in giving results, it is said that the cure is

permanent and without any side effects. Homeopathic remedies are typically derived from plants, herbs, minerals or animal products.

<u>Biochemic tissue salts</u> – These are minerals such as rock salt that have been prepared using the homeopathic method. There are 12 tissue salts in total. William Heinrich Schuessler was a German medical doctor and Naturopath. He concocted 12 biochemic "cell salts" or "tissue salts" intended to redress perceived bodily deficiencies in one mineral or another. He believed that a human body is made of these 12 salts. Schuessler believed that tissue salts could restore mineral deficiencies that made the body susceptible to illness.

<u>Surgery/Operation</u> – It is a medical specialty that uses operative techniques on a patient to investigate or treat a pathological condition such as a disease or injury to help improve bodily function. For example if a female patient has breast cancer, then one way to cure it could be removal of that breast by surgical operation.

<u>Bach Flower Remedies</u> – Bach flower essences are extracts from flowers which have a positive effect on emotional imbalances and mood swings such as fear, dejection, lack of self-confidence, stress and worrying. The name comes from Dr Edward Bach (1886-1936) who discovered this healing method. For more than 70 years these flower essences have proved useful for children as well as adults for all kinds of emotional problems. There are about 38 Bach flowers whose essence is captured in liquid

form. 4 drops of each essence or a mix of various essences as required depending on the symptoms is given to the patient. It is really amazing to see how this system of medicine works.

CHAPTER 33

VALUE ADDED TAX

Sales tax was an old taxying system applied to purchases of goods or services and other taxable supplies. In this system, it was clearly the consumer who paid all the tax. The raw material Seller or the Manufacturer did not pay any tax directly to the Government. It was the Retailer who charged the Consumer 10% Sales Tax and sent it to the Government. The Retailer did not pay any tax out of his own earned money. He was merely acting as a conveyer of the tax collected from the Consumer to the Government. The only person who directly paid all the tax was the Consumer.

In the new tax system called the Value Added Tax (VAT) System, the Government has ensured that some amount of tax is paid by everyone. So the raw material Seller charges 10% tax to the Manufacturer and gives it to the Government. The Manufacturer charges 10% tax to the Retailor and gives it to the Government minus the tax that he has paid to the raw material Seller. The Retailor charges 10% tax to the Consumer and gives it to the Government minus the tax that he has paid to the Manufacturer. Thus in this system Government collects tax at every stage of transaction of the goods.

You will be surprised to know that even with this System there is no material change in what money the Consumer pays as tax or in what the Government gets as overall tax or as Profit that the Manufacturer or the Retailor gets as compared to the earlier Sales Tax System. Let us take an example to prove what has been said so far.

<u>Old Tax System</u>

Consider the manufacture and sale of any item, which in this case we will call as Object. Consider that the Object manufacturer spends Rs 100/- on purchase of raw material from the Raw Material Seller and uses it to make the Object. The Object is then sold wholesale to a Retailer for Rs 120/- making a profit of Rs 20/- The Retailer then sells it to a Consumer for Rs 150 + 15 (150 x 10% Sales Tax) = Rs 165 and pays the Govt Rs 15/- thus making a profit of Rs30/-

So the consumer has paid 10% (Rs 15/-) extra, and the government has collected this amount in taxation. The retailers have not paid any tax directly (it is only the consumer who has paid the tax), but the retailer has to do the paperwork in order to correctly pass on to the government the sales tax it has collected. Suppliers and Manufacturers only have the administrative burden of supplying correct certifications, and checking that their retailers aren't consumers.

VAT System

Vat is consumption tax levied on products at every point of sale where value has been added starting from raw materials and going all the way to the final retail purchase. Ultimately the consumer pays vat. Buyers at every stage of production receive reimbursements for the previous vat they have paid.

In value added tax System, With a 10% VAT, the calculations will be as follows:-

The manufacturer pays Rs 110 (Rs 100 + 10% of Rs 100 as tax = Rs 110) for the raw materials, and the seller of the raw materials pays the government Rs 10 as tax.

The manufacturer charges the retailer Rs120 + (10% of Rs120 as tax) = Rs132 and pays the government 10% of 120 =12 minus Rs 10 which he has already paid as tax to seller. Thus, he pays Rs 2 getting the same profit of Rs 20. (132 – 2 – 110 = 20).

The retailer charges the consumer Rs 150 + (10% of Rs 150 as tax) = Rs165 and pays the government Rs 3 (Rs 15 - 12 which he has paid to manufacturer), thus getting the same profit of Rs 30 as in earlier Sales Tax System. (Rs 165 - 3 - 132 = Rs 30).

In VAT System Govt share of Taxes is Rs 10 (From raw material seller) + Rs 2 (from Manufacturer) + Rs 3 (From Retailer) = total Rs 15, same as in old Sales Tax System. Also, the total price of the Object and tax incurred by the Consumer as Rs 165 is same as in the old Sales Tax

System. Also the profit made by the Manufacturer of Rs 20 and Retailer of Rs 30 is the same.

In VAT system, as compared to other tax systems, there is a less chance of tax evasion. Vat is simple to administer as compared to Sales Tax System. In VAT, the incidence of cascading is avoided as the tax is imposed on the value addition at every stage of production. Vat system encourages payment of taxes and discourages attempts to avoid them.

One of the disadvantages is that it is not a simple task to calculate value added at every stage. All purchases and sales records need to be maintained which causes increase in compliance cost.

Years back when Sales Tax System was in force, I went to buy a pair of shoes and I remember the cashier asking me whether I wanted a Bill. He said to me that if I insisted on a bill, the shoes will cost me Rs 220 but if I don't take a bill, he can give me 5% discount. Obviously he intended to pocket the other 5%. How clever of him and dumb of people like me who didn't insist on getting a bill !!

CHAPTER 34

MEANINGLESS WORDS

There are thousands of languages spoken in our world and many more dialects. In almost all the languages we use certain words which we actually don't mean. They appear in colloquial language and not in formal written language. Some such words spoken in English language are given below.

The first such word that comes to my mind is "Really". Just to keep the conversation going and to tell the speaker that he is being heard, the listener often uses these words, "Oh really". Another such conjunctive word is, "Oh, don't tell me!!". Actually you want him to tell you more but these words are used to show surprise and to convey to the speaker that you are a careful listener. There are more such words used without actually meaning them like "You don't say!!", "Oh my God!!"

Then there is a word "Sorry" which is used profusely by many without actually feeling sorry. For instance if a person is saying something and he makes a mistake, he quickly ends up saying "Sorry" or "Pardon Me". These words have become like conjunctions. The person using these words is actually not feeling sorry or begging you to pardon him. Another example - when the lift door opens the person outside wants to get in and the one inside wants to come out and they confront each other both saying, "Oh sorry".

Then there are words like "You know", "I know" which are used profusely during conversation. For example when a person is talking about his trip to say US, the conversation might proceed something like this, "You know, I had gone to US and the weather was awful". "I know" says the listener who actually doesn't know when his friend had gone to US. "You know, there I came across an Indian Restaurant". Instead of saying Ok or is it? he again says "I know". "You know, that restaurant was very good". "I know". "You know, it made me feel home sick". "I know". "You know, the Dosa and other preparations were superb". "I know". And the conversation just carries on in this manner.

Many spoken sentences start with "You know". You know it's crazy. You know it's beautiful. You know people go crazy watching him. You know it's absolutely horrific. And many more You knows.

I heard an interview being given by a cricket captain. I was counting the number of times he used the words "You know". He started like this, "You know, we are playing here for the first time. You know, it's very cold here. My guys are not used to this kind of weather. You know, they suffer from stiffness of muscles and you know it affects their game" and he carried on using many more "You Knows". Yes, it was amusing to count the number of times that he used the words "You know".

Then there is a fellow who wants to be very honest about what he is saying. "You know, to be honest I liked the movie. I liked everybody's acting. You know to be honest, the story has been written very well. Even the Director has done a good job. To be honest you must see it to believe it". And he carries on showing his honesty in every sentence. Funny fellow!!

CHAPTER 35

HUSBAND'S APPLICATION TO WIFE

Dear Senior Male Citizens, this application which I am writing from a good old husband to his dear wife will be applicable to most of you. Please put your wife's name at the beginning of the application and then put your name at the end and send it without a second thought. Believe me, you won't regret. I promise you that you will enjoy a comfortable sleep thereafter. So here we go.

My dear so & so,

I really love you and I know that you too love me immensely. I am reminded of the good old days when we married and for want of proper accommodation and furniture, how we enjoyed sleeping on a single bed and sharing one blanket. Some years later we got a double bed to sleep on and a double blanket too. Some years later, it became a tug of war with the blanket. Thinking logically and to avoid fights, we found a way out and ended the tug of war by deciding to sleep in two single blankets. That gave us some peace and we started enjoying our sleep again.

Now we have added more years to our lives. And now I have realised that my body has started failing me. Many of my body organs are getting weak and I have started suffering from body ache, acidity and lot of gases. I feel that

I am being unfair by making you bear with all my problems. When I am lying down in the same bed and in the same room, I feel very scared to roll around and change my side because the bed makes noise which can wake you up. So no matter how much my aching body wants me to turn around, I control myself. Yet another dilemma which I face is to get up and go to the toilet to pass my urine. Unfortunately the muscles in the bladder have lost their strength and I get frequent calls to visit the toilet. I feel very worried that your sleep might get disturbed but instead of urinating in the bed, I try and go to the toilet with least possible noise.

Another big problem which is created by the gases which the stomach generates, is that these gases want to come out from both ends. No matter how hard I try, to hold them back, they finally win. And the more I try to hold them back, the more loudly they come out. All these problems with the gases, body ache, snoring, coughing, sneezing is ruining my sleep.

Dear so & so, may I request you to be reasonable and help to find a solution. The best solution that comes to my mind is that I shift into another bed room. My shifting in another room is definitely not going to decrease my love and fondness for you. Remember how we took a good decision earlier and changed from one double blanket to two single blankets and enjoyed better sleep thereafter, similarly my shifting from this bed room to another separate bed room will certainly help us to sleep better. Both of us will enjoy our sleep and get up in good state of mind which I am sure will certainly have a good effect on reducing the verbal fights that we have. On trial basis we could do this for ten odd days and then take a final decision. Please do think over my proposal and let me know.

Love you more than ever

Put your Name

Send this application and enjoy undisturbed snoring and farting and also enjoy an excellent night sleep in the separate room.

CHAPTER 36

LOVE THYSELF

My daughter was about 5 yrs old. My mother was about 90 yrs old. She was putting on years but losing life gradually whereas the daughter was putting on years and adding life to those years. Both used to behave in more or less in a similar way.

One day, jokingly my mother asked her, "Beta whom do you like the most, your Mom, or your Dad, or Me?" The answer that the 5 yr old gave was brilliant. She took a minute posing as if she was thinking and finally said, "Grandma, I like myself the most".

Her answer really shook me. I don't think that the little girl knew what diplomacy meant. She couldn't have thought that if she mentioned one out of the three, the other two will feel hurt. And so I surmised that her answer must be genuine. There is a lot to learn from that answer. Though all of us love our life the most, we don't think of it that way on a daily basis and that is why we abuse our body without bothering about the consequences.

I have seen dog owners loving their dog the most - more than their spouse or even their children and they are ready to sacrifice anything for the happiness of their dog. When they enter the house, the first creature they hug is the dog and then other family members. That is because as soon as they enter the house, the dog comes running and jumping and wanting to climb all over the owner demanding his love in return. They sacrifice their morning sleep to take the dog for a walk. They ensure that they get proper meal for the dog. But ultimately, when it comes to it, they love their life more than the dog's life.

"Loving yourself the most" would that be selfish? No, I don't think so. We all know that life is dear to everyone. It is more dear than one's spouse or even children. It is just that we don't give adequate thought to this fact on daily basis. The fact that all creatures love their life the most has been beautifully demonstrated by Birbal to King Akbar when he asked Birbal, "Tell me, what is the most loved thing to a person?" Birbal made a mother monkey stand in a pool of water with her baby standing next to her. He then slowly started raising the water level. As the water level started crossing the height of the baby, the mother lifted the baby in her arms. When the water level came up to her neck, she lifted the baby above her head. As the water level rose further and she started drowning, Akbar was most surprised to see the mother monkey put the child below her feet to rise a little higher to save her life. What an amazing way to demonstrate that life is a most dear thing to everyone.

CHAPTER 37

UTILITY

Utility as a word can be defined as a state of being useful, profitable or beneficial. As an Adjective, it means usefulness, especially through being able to perform several functions eg a utility truck or utility clothing like Jeans more functional than attractive. Economic utility of an object means value that one can get from it. Thus the word "Utility" can be used in many ways.

Time is one factor which in many cases reduces the utility of an object. For example a brand new Mixer has very high utility but with passage of time, as it gets old, its utility (usefulness) reduces. Similarly a new car has very high utility initially but with passage of time as it gets unreliable, its utility decreases.

This word utility can also be affected by change in existing situation. The effect can be either to decrease or even increase. This word utility can also be applied to humans. It may sound a bit harsh, but Gandhiji's utility as a leader pre-independence was very high. But some feel that after we got independence his utility was decreasing rapidly. They feel that Gandhi was too accommodative to Muslims during the partition of India. An example of this was regarding payment to Pakistan. The Govt of India led by Congress leaders had withheld a payment to Pak in Jan

1948 because it did not want to finance Pak which was at war with India over Kashmir at that time. Gandhi opposed the decision to freeze the payment and went on a fast-unto-death on 13 Jan 48 to pressurise the Indian Govt to release the payment. The Indian Govt yielding to Gandhi's pressure reversed its decision. This was interpreted by Nathuram Godse and his colleagues as Gandhi controlling power and selling India to Muslims. They could feel that Gandhi was causing more harm than good to India. And therefore they started the plan of assassinating Gandhi.

The concreate plans to assassinate Gandhi were initiated by Godse and his accomplices in 1948. The team consisted of 9 people with Narayan Vinayak Godse and Narayan Apte as the main planners. Nathuram Godse shot Gandhi on 30 Jan 1948. Godse and Apte were hanged in Ambala jail on 15 Nov 1949.

CHAPTER 38

EUTHANASIA

"Euthanasia" is defined as painless killing of a patient suffering from an incurable and painful disease or an irreversible coma. Euthanasia in Greek language means "good death". It is the practice of intentionally ending a life to relieve pain and suffering.

Euthanasia is also called mercy killing. It is an act or practice of painlessly putting to death persons suffering from painful and incurable disease or incapacitating physical disorder. Because there is no specific provision for it in most legal systems, it is usually regarded as either abetment of suicide or murder if performed by another person.

There are several types of Euthanasia. Two main types are Active and Passive. When a doctor purposefully gives someone a lethal dose of a sedative, it is considered as Active euthanasia. Passive euthanasia is sometimes described as intentionally withholding artificial life support such as ventilator or feeding tube.

The first countries to legalise Euthanasia were Netherlands in 2001 and Belgium in 2003. Active euthanasia is legal in Netherlands, Belgium, Columbia, Luxembourg and Canada. Assisted suicide, meaning suicide that is assisted by a physician who writes a prescription for a lethal dose of drugs but does not give it himself, is legal in Switzerland, Germany, Australian state of Victoria and in parts of US.

In India passive euthanasia has been made legal since March 2018 under strict guidelines which state that Patients must consent through a "living will" and must be either terminally ill or in vegetative state.

"Living Will" is a legal document in which a healthy person with sound mind and memory specifies what actions should be taken for his health if he is no longer able to make decisions for himself because of illness or incapacity.

Now that we understand to some extent what euthanasia means, let us take some examples and see what is your opinion regarding them.

<u>First Example</u> – A young bachelor man has a two wheeler accident and has a severe head injury and goes into a state of coma. He remains in coma during the next 10 years. When asked by his father about the doctor's opinion regarding his getting back to normal, the doctor mentioned that nothing can be said with certainty, he may or may not recover. The parents were going through hard time to meet the hospital expenditure and also bearing the mental torture. So, what is your opinion? Does he qualify for euthanasia?

<u>Second Example</u> – An old man aged 95 years who has no disease, is constantly asking GOD, "Oh God, have you forgotten me? When will you call me to serve you? You

have already taken away my wife and all my friends. I am really tired and fed up of living here. I have done all my duties. Now there is nothing left to do. Please call me and release me from this punishment. Living through each day is very painful". Do you think this case qualifies for euthanasia?

<u>Third Example</u> – Husband and wife were driving in a car. They have an accident in which the wife gets paralysed waist downwards. She can move around only in a wheel chair. For 10 years she lives with the hope that technology will help her to get artificial legs. But finally it becomes clear to her that technology cannot help her and that she will have to live like this at the mercy of her husband. That's when she begs her husband to take up her case for mercy killing. What is your opinion?

These are only three examples out of many that I have quoted. I am all for euthanasia. Keeping legal aspects out, I feel that we should study each case on its merit and permit mercy killing. At the end, we all have to die so why not make death easy. When a pet dog gets old, keeping all our love for it aside, don't we relieve the dog by resorting to active euthanasia?

CHAPTER 39

VERBAL DIARRHOEA

Her name was Rajani. She was a compulsive talker meaning she had to talk continuously right from the time she got out of her bed. Her husband was fed up of her talking. He preferred to have atleast 30 minutes of peace after getting up so that he could meditate for 15 minutes and then plan his day. But his wife wouldn't let him do that. He tried to get up half an hour early but his wife used to sense his early getting up and also get up early and start off saying for instance, "Is everything fine darling or have you got an upset tummy? If gases are troubling you then please take four tablets of Natrum Phos. It is an excellent biochemic medicine for relieving gases. Do you know that our body is made up of 12 biochemic salts and if the body experiences deficiency of any salt then it suffers from some ailment. And she just carried on and on and on----". Thanks to a mobile call which she got that spared him. He knew that for atleast next thirty minutes she will be busy with that call and he will remain undisturbed in the next room.

One day I asked my friend, "Well, how are things?" to which he replied saying, "Things are really bad friend. I am unable to get time for myself when I am alone with my wife. I am just not able to put in even one word in the conversation. I think she suffers from Verbal Diarrhoea to which there seems to be no medicine".

I asked him, "What do you mean by Verbal Diarrhoea?" His reply was, "We generally relate Diarrhoea to frequent loose, watery bowel movements. Well, in case of my wife I relate it her loose, slippery tongue which has no control. Once she starts, there is no stopping. She doesn't bother whether I am listening to her or not. In any case, when she is talking, she cannot hear a word. She can talk to any thing, even a mirror or a wall.

I will give you a classic example of her Verbal Diarrhoea. One day she gave a call to one of her friends. When the call was picked up, the subsequent conversation went like so, "Can I speak to Vibha?" Reply came saying, "Sorry, there is no Vibha here". She didn't give up and said, "OK I am Rajani. I am staying in Pashan. It is a green zone. By the way where are you staying? Is your area red?" The Wrong Number replied, "I am staying in Model Colony. It is red in some areas. Fortunately where I am staying, it is green". Rajani's reply was - "Wow great. Lot of people are being affected by Corona virus. Hope you are taking good care. I am staying with my husband in a flat – just two of us. We have two daughters. Both are away, the elder is in US and the younger one in UK. How about your family?"

My friend said that he went close to his wife and whispered in her ear "Whom are you talking to?" His wife covered the speaker and said, "Some wrong number"! She then re-joined her conversation with the wrong number and said, "My husband was wanting to know whom was I talking to. Can you give me your name if you don't mind". The wrong number said, "I am Sheela Paranjape. I am staying with my husband and two children". Rajani said, "Oh, that's great. Hope you are enjoying the lock down and the opportunity that you have got to talk to your family members". And there conversation carried on and on and on. Probably the lady with that Wrong Number also had some amount of Verbal Diarrhoea.

I gave a serious thought to this situation. From my experience, I have noticed that after a gathering is over, the men walk out while the women keep talking even after saying Bye. While leaving, why do women love to talk at the door and near the lift? I have noticed that most women talk far too much as compared to the men particularly the older women. With age, the men start talking less and less because they start realising that there is no point in talking. But with age, the older women start talking more and more – why so? What do you have to say?